About the Author

Barbara Cartland, the world's most famous romantic novelist, who is also an historian, playwright, lecturer, political speaker and television personality, has now written over 460 books and sold nearly 500 million copies all over the world.

She has also had many historical works published and has written four autobiographies as well as the biographies of her mother and that of her brother, Ronald Cartland, who was the first Member of Parliament to be killed in the last war. This book has a preface by Sir Winston Churchill and has just been republished with an introduction by the late Sir Arthur Bryant.

Love at the Helm, a novel written with the help and inspiration of the late Earl Mountbatten of Burma, Great Uncle of His Royal Highness The Prince of Wales, is being sold for the Mountbatten Memorial Trust.

She has broken the world record for the last twelve years by writing an average of twenty-three books a year. In the Guinness Book of Records she is listed as the world's top-selling author.

Miss Cartland in 1978 sang an Album of Love Songs with the Royal Philharmonic orchestra.

In private life Barbara Cartland, who is a Dame of Grace of the Order of St John of Jerusalem, Chairman of the St John Council in Hertfordshire and Deputy President of the St John Ambulance Brigade, has fought for better conditions and salaries for Midwives and Nurses.

She championed the cause for the Elderly in 1956 invoking a Government Enquiry into the "Housing Conditions of Old People".

In 1962 she had the Law of England changed so that Local Authorities had to provide camps for their own Gypsies. This has meant that since then thousands and thousands of Gypsy children have been able to go to School which they had never been able to do in the past, as their caravans were moved every twenty-four hours by the Police.

There are now fourteen camps in Hertfordshire and Barbara Cartland has her own Romany Gypsy Camp called Barbaraville by the Gypsies.

Her designs "Decorating with Love" are being sold all over the USA and the National Home Fashions League made her, in 1981, "Woman of Achievement".

Barbara Cartland's book *Getting Older, Growing Younger* has been published in Great Britain and the USA and her fifth Cookery Book, *The Romance of Food*, is now being used by the House of Commons.

In 1984 she received at Kennedy Airport, America's Bishop Wright Air Industry Award for her contribution to the development of aviation. In 1931 she and two R.A.F. Officers thought of, and carried the first aeroplane-towed glider air-mail.

During the War she was Chief Lady Welfare Officer in Bedfordshire looking after 20,000 Service men and women. She thought of having a pool of Wedding Dresses at the War Office so a Service Bride could hire a gown for the day.

She bought 1,000 gowns without coupons for the A.T.S., the W.A.A.F.s and the W.R.E.N.S. In 1945 Barbara Cartland received the Certificate of Merit from Eastern Command.

In 1964 Barbara Cartland founded the National Association for Health of which she is the President, as a front for all the Health Stores and for any product made as alternative medicine.

This has now a £500,000,000 turnover a year, with one third going in export.

In January 1988 she received "La Medaille de Vermeil de la Ville de Paris" (the Gold Medal of the City of Paris). This is the highest award to be given by the City of Paris for ACHIEVEMENT – 25 million books sold in France.

THE PASSIONATE PRINCESS

When Princess Thea is told by her father the King of Kostas that she has to marry the Monarch of a neighbouring State she is horrified.

King Otto may be important to Kostas, but he is very old.

Fired by her dreams of love, she runs away and finds, high in the mountains among the fir trees an Artist called Niklōs.

She realises instinctively that he is the man who is the other half of herself, and he feels the same.

They can read each other's thoughts, they have a closeness which sweeps away everything else and she stays in his little house on the side of a mountain.

How Niklōs takes Thea to hear the music of the Gypsies. How on the way home they are captured by a band of ferocious Bandits who have terrified all the countries in the Balkans. How Niklōs saves Thea from two lecherous younger Bandits and how in the darkness of a cave he asks her to be his wife – is all told in this thrilling story of a wild, passionate love – the 413th book by BARBARA CARTLAND.

BARBARA CARTLAND

THE PASSIONATE PRINCESS

Pan Original
Pan Books London, Sydney and Auckland

First published 1988 by Pan Books Ltd,
Cavaye Place, London SW10 9PG

9 8 7 6 5 4 3 2 1

© Cartland Promotions 1988

ISBN 0 330 30469 0

Phototypeset by Input Typesetting Ltd, London SW19 8DR

Printed and bound in Great Britain by
Richard Clay Ltd, Bungay, Suffolk

AUTHOR'S NOTE

Hungarians are passionate, romantic and wild underneath a charming exterior. The very intensity and strength of their feelings exemplifies their characters and their outlook on life.

They are a bewildering people to outsiders. They have an enormous capacity for enjoyment and tenacious friendships. They are easy-going, but once they are roused, nothing will stop them.

For a political or national cause a Magyar will do anything. Love of his country is impregnated into his very being, and at its call will arouse him to sublime sacrifice.

Music, like love, is in their blood. For generations the Gypsies have stirred the souls of man with their music.

The *Csárdás*, a tavern dance, originated in the nineteenth century. The Gypsy beauty, the Gypsy madness, the fierce passion, the unutterable sadness, the love and rage, is all to be found in it.

Among the peasants, the black magic of the Gypsy is far more potent in cases of real need than the supernatural powers claimed by the priests.

Chapter One
1870

Princess Thea was singing as she walked along the passage and went down a secondary staircase.

She was thinking as she did so that it was annoying that the best part of the Palace was always kept for Royal Receptions.

She enjoyed the Grand Staircase with its gilt and crystal balustrade.

She loved the pictures on the walls and the magnificent marble mantelpieces which had been sculpted by Italian craftsmen.

It was her great-grandfather who had made the Palace one of the most impressive in the Balkans.

He had felt, the Princess always thought, that it was a compensation for Kostas being as a country so small and comparatively unimportant.

She often thought that he had had what was really an inferiority complex.

He had insisted on always being surrounded by all the pomp and grandeur that went with Monarchy.

He had even expounded such ideas to his grandchildren and Princess Thea had been christened Sydel Niobe Anthea.

She had however, repudiated such a mouthful from the moment she could speak.

She referred to herself as 'Thea'. The name had stuck and no one in the family had called her anything else.

She went into the Breakfast-Room.

It was a quite pleasant but not impressive room which caught the morning sun.

She found her brother Georgi having his breakfast.

He looked up as his sister came into the room and said:

"You are late!"

"Yes, I know," Thea replied, "but it was so lovely this morning and *Mercury* took all the jumps as if he was flying!"

She helped herself to one of the dishes of what was a very English breakfast on the sideboard.

Her father, King Alpheus of Kostas, had spent quite a lot of his time when he was a young man in England.

He had actually taken a Degree at Oxford University.

He therefore imitated quite a lot of English ways and he insisted that his children spoke English.

This was not difficult for Thea and Georgi as they had learnt the languages of all the surrounding Balkan countries.

Georgi had once said that after some of those, English was 'a piece of cake'!

Carrying her plate, Thea sat down at the table.

Her mind was still on her ride.

As she picked up her knife and fork she said:

"By the way, the fences should be higher."

"I know that," her brother replied. "You had better see to it."

"Why me?"

"I am going away tomorrow."

"Going away?" his sister exclaimed. "But why, and where?"

Georgi looked over his shoulder.

"As it happens," he said, "I am going to Paris. You

must not tell Mama! She thinks I am paying a semi-State Visit to the French Army."

"You are going to Paris again?" Thea said. "I cannot think why you do not stay here."

Her brother smiled.

"I can give you one answer to that – Paris is extremely amusing and the women are fantastic!"

Thea stared at him.

"You mean you are just going to enjoy yourself?"

"That about sums it up in a nutshell!"

"And you are going . . alone?"

"I shall not be alone for long!"

"Take me . . with you! Please . . take me with you!" Thea pleaded.

"You can hear Mama agreeing to that!" Georgi scoffed.

"But . . surely we could . . say I was . . staying with one of your friends?"

"Mama would certainly not approve of that!"

"Why not?"

"Because they are fascinating and very attractive, but certainly not the right companions for a well-brought-up Princess!"

Thea made a sound of disgust.

"Why could I not have been a boy?"

"You will find quite a lot of men will be glad you are a girl!"

Thea looked at him derisively.

"Men?" she asked. "Where do I see them, except for the old Courtiers who are practically falling into the grave!"

Her brother poured himself out some more coffee.

"You have a point there," he said. "But, as it happens, Papa is arranging your marriage. He was talking to me about it last night."

Now Thea was stunned.

"My . . marriage?" she repeated in a low voice.

"You are eighteen," her brother said, "and Papa thinks that you must enhance the importance of our country by a alliance with one of our more distinguished neighbours."

"Who?" Thea asked abruptly.

"It seems likely to be King Otho of Kanaris."

There was a horrified silence until Thea asked:

"Are . . you . . serious?"

"There does not appear to be anybody else."

"But . . he is old . . much older than . . Papa!"

"His country is twice the size of ours."

"But . . how can I possibly . . marry an old man like that? When I saw him . . last his hair and his beard were . . white!"

"It is a bit hard on you," her brother conceded, "but – you have to marry someone!"

"I . . I want to marry someone young . . with whom I am . . in love!"

Georgi sat back in his chair.

"You know as well as I do, Thea, because we are Royal, we have to take what is available, think of our country first and ourselves last!"

"If that is what you really think, then why do you not marry?" Thea enquired.

There was silence. Then her brother said:

"I know it has to happen sometime, and Papa is already looking around. She is sure to be plain, fat and deadly dull!"

He spoke violently and added:

"That is why I want to go to Paris. I intend to enjoy myself while I can!"

There was a harshness in the way he spoke.

Then she said in a small voice:

"Must . . I do . . this?"

"You know the answer to that," her brother replied.

"There must be . . somebody better than . . King Otho!"

"That is what I said to Papa last night," Georgi replied, "but he pointed out that practically every one of our neighbours is either married with six children, or a widower like King Otho, or a misogynist, like King Ápád."

"What is a misogynist?" Thea enquired.

"A man who hates women," her brother replied. "It usually happens when a man has had an unfortunate love-affair which leaves him cynical and bitter."

"But . . there must be . . someone . . else!" Thea said desperately.

"I am sorry, old girl," Georgi said, "but I did go through the possibilities with Papa, and we came up with nothing."

"It is unfair!" Thea cried. "I will not . . marry him! I shall . . refuse!"

She spoke violently.

She knew in her heart that if there was no alternative it was something she would have to do.

She was aware that her father's obsession with improving the status of Kostas would make him obstinate. Nothing she could say would have any effect.

She stared across the table at Georgi and there were tears in her eyes as she said pleadingly:

"Help me . . Georgi . . please . . help me!"

"I only wish I could," Georgi replied, "but I am in the same boat as you are! I shall be twenty-two next month, and Papa has told me I have to be married by next year and start to provide more heirs to the throne."

Thea got up from the breakfast-table.

"The whole . . idea makes me . . sick!"

She walked to the window to look out at the well-laid-out garden that was bright with Spring flowers.

What she was really seeing however was the lined face of King Otho.

His white hair growing thin on the top of his head.

She had never imagined, never thought for one moment, that she would have to marry a man like that.

Because she had been so much alone when Georgi was at school, and then in the Army, she read Fairy-Stories.

She believed them. They were part of her very existence.

She had dreamt that one day a tall, handsome Prince would come into her life.

They would fall in love and be married.

He would understand how much the beauty of the countryside meant to her, the high mountains with their snowy peaks which enclosed Kostas.

The silver river which ran through the valley and fed the verdant fields on either side of it.

The peasants were poor but there was always plenty of fruit and vegetables and the women were noted for their lovely skins.

Kostas lay on the Southern border of Hungary.

Their blood had been mixed over the centuries which accounted for many of the women having red hair which was characteristic of the Hungarians.

Thea's hair was red. It was not the dark auburn shade which was common in Austria.

It was rather a mixture of red and gold which in the sunshine made her hair like dancing flames.

It was inevitable that her eyes should be green.

When she was upset they seemed to have a dark, almost purple tinge in them.

She had no idea that her brother was watching her.

He was thinking how Thea had in the last year, developed into a beauty.

She would grow even lovelier as she grew older.

It was a pity that there was no one more suitable for her as a husband than King Otho but there was however nothing he could do about it.

He had in fact, done his best.

14

He had argued with his father until in exasperation the King had said:

"Do not be more of a fool than you are usually! We are not important enough to be considered by the Royalty of larger countries!"

His voice was harsh as he said:

"Nor has Thea a large enough dowry to attract them!"

Georgi was aware that was always a sore point that his father had never had as much money as he required.

This was partly due to the ambitious schemes of his father.

He had spent an inordinate amount of money building the Palace and laying out the grounds.

He had also provided their small Army with colourful and elaborate uniforms as well as up-to-date guns which they never used.

Unless they found gold in the mountains or pearls in the river, which was unlikely, Georgi knew they would have to struggle on, trying to make ends meet.

He was therefore aware that his father was looking for a Princess with money for him.

It did not matter whether she was fat, thin, plain or pretty; if her dowry was big enough he would have to accept her.

It was the thought of being saddled with such a wife that had made him rush to Paris.

There the fascinating Courtesans might be expensive, but they knew how to make a man forget.

He was thinking of how enjoyable it had been the last time.

He knew there were several alluring *filles de joie* who would welcome him with open arms.

It was not only because he was a Prince or that somehow he managed to pay them.

He was an extremely good-looking young man. What

was more, the men of Kostas were noted for being fascinating and ardent lovers.

This too was something they had inherited from Hungary and the fact also that they were brilliant horsemen.

Georgi rose from his chair and walked towards his sister.

He put his arm around her shoulders and said:

"Cheer up, old girl! When we are both married, I will make some excuse to take you to Paris, or perhaps to England with me."

Thea was listening and he added:

"A married woman has far more licence than a young girl."

"I want to . . come with . . you now."

"I wish I could take you," Georgi replied, "but I expect you would be shocked, and it would considerably 'cramp my style'!"

Thea accepted this.

Then she said in a very small voice:

"You . . you do not think Papa . . would do . . anything while . . you are away?"

"If I get the chance I will persuade him not to," Georgi promised. "At the same time, I do not want him to make it an excuse to cancel my trip."

Thea gave a deep sigh.

"No . . of course . . not."

"What you have to do," her brother went on, "is to enjoy yourself while you can. Raise the fences and ride while you still do not have to be accompanied."

Thea gasped.

"Do you mean . . if I am . . married . . I shall have to have some . . dreary Lady-in-Waiting or an *Aide-de-camp* with me?"

Georgi did not reply and she knew the answer.

Of course, as a Queen she would be hedged about as if she was a prisoner.

They were somewhat understaffed at the Palace.

She therefore had been allowed to ride alone in the Park without having a groom always in attendance.

It was understood that she did not go outside the walls which encircled the Park.

There she could be alone, she could think, she could talk to Mercury without being overheard.

Now she began to consider the horror of being so important that she could not be alone.

It would be different, she thought, if she could ride with somebody she loved. Someone she could talk to.

In the stories she told herself her dream-man, who was "Prince Charming", was always a magnificent rider.

They would have horses that were so fine and so spirited that no one could keep up with them.

They would ride away alone, into an indefinite horizon.

Thinking of King Otho, she felt quite certain that he was not a good rider. Certainly not an outstanding one.

She was sure he would also be very particular about protocol.

She had tried not to listen to her Governesses when they said to her:

"A *Princess* does not do this – a *Princess* does not do that!" "You must remember, Your Royal Highness, that you are a *Princess*!"

Now she was certain the same thing would be said by her husband.

It would be exactly the same, except that it would be:

"A *Queen* does not do anything she wants to do."

As if Georgi knew what she was thinking, he gave her a hug and said:

"I have to go now. I am accompanying Papa on a Parade which is exactly like the one he took last week, and the week before that!"

"But you will be free tomorrow?" Thea asked.

"Thank God for small mercies!" her brother replied. "Even though, as you well know, they are very small and very short."

He walked out of the Breakfast-Room as he spoke but Thea did not follow him.

Instead she continued to look blindly out of the window and every part of her body was crying out in horror.

When finally she went to the Music-Room where her teacher was waiting, she was very pale.

Her Governesses had been dispensed with as soon as she had reached the age of eighteen.

There were however certain teachers who came from outside the Palace and with those she continued her studies.

Her favourite was the old Professor who taught her music.

He had been a great success all over Europe before he had retired.

It was the Queen who had been clever enough to realise that he could be just the sort of teacher for her daughter.

The Professor taught Thea to express herself in the way she played, and in the compositions she wrote.

She tried to translate into her music the beauty which made her heart leap when she looked at it.

She listened to the sounds of the birds, then she expressed on the piano, the joy in their voices.

When she went into the Music-Room the Professor was sitting at the piano.

He was playing a soft dreamy Waltz which was very romantic.

It made Thea think of the 'Prince Charming' that she had believed one day she would find.

Then with an almost brutal sense of reality she remembered he was King Otho.

18

The Professor greeted her and she sat down at the piano.

She began to play of the terror, misery and the sense of revolt she felt at what was waiting for her.

It was not until the evening that Thea received a message from her father.

His Chief *Aide-de-camp* was a middle-aged man who had served the King for many years.

He came to her Sitting-Room to say:

"His Majesty has asked me to inform Your Royal Highness that he wishes to see you in his Study."

Thea had been reading, and thought almost clairvoyantly that this was the moment of Doom.

She had prayed that her father would delay what he had to say to her until Georgi returned from Paris.

She had clung to her brother's assurance that he would ask him to do so.

She was aware now that because the King was always impatient, he wanted to get on with the whole arrangement.

'Before I know where I am,' she thought, 'I shall be up the aisle and married.'

She wondered if she could tell the *Aide-de-camp* that she was too tired and too unwell to obey her father's summons.

Then she knew that if she did so, she would be unable to ride tomorrow.

Mercury would be waiting for her, and she thought wildly that only her horse would understand what she was feeling.

"I also have to tell Your Royal Highness," the *Aide-de-camp* was saying, "that Prince Georgi changed his plans at the last moment and decided to leave for Paris this evening."

19

"You mean . . he has already . . gone?" Thea asked in astonishment.

"His Royal Highness only just had time to catch the Express. He asked me to say goodbye to you."

Without being told, Thea knew exactly what had happened.

Georgi had asked their father to do nothing about her marriage until he returned.

The King had refused, and her brother had therefore run away.

She knew he disliked any sort of scene, especially recriminations.

He had therefore taken the easy way out and she did not blame him.

She only knew he had accepted the inevitable.

He knew there was nothing he could do about it.

Slowly she put down her book and rose to her feet.

"Please tell His Majesty that I will be with him in a few minutes," she said.

The *Aide-de-camp* bowed and left the room.

Thea walked to where hanging on the wall was a mirror in an elaborate gold frame surmounted by cupids.

She stared at her reflection. Then she asked aloud:

"Mirror, mirror, tell me true,
Help me, tell me what to do!"

She almost expected the mirror to reply but instead there was only the reflection of herself.

Her small oval face, her straight little nose, and her large green eyes.

The last light of the setting sun turned her hair to flaming gold.

Then with a sound that was half a groan and half a sob she turned from the mirror and she went out of the room and down the stairs.

Her father's Study was a very comfortable room.

Unlike the gilt-framed, tapestry-covered furniture in

the main part of the Palace, the King had big, comfortable leather arm-chairs.

The sofa was as soft as a feather-bed, and a large flat-topped desk was easy to write on.

The pictures in the room were all of his ancestors.

Their frames were carved and gilded, and each one was surmounted by a crown.

There were also, because the King appreciated them, some fine Chinese vases.

In each one there was an arrangement of purple and white lilac and syringa.

The whole room, Thea had often thought, expressed the many different facets of her father's character.

At the same time she was aware that it was impossible not to look at the enormous Royal insignia carved and painted in gold and brilliant colours which hung over the mantelpiece.

Sitting at his desk the King looked directly at them.

She thought they reminded him every day, every hour and every minute, of his responsibilities towards his Kingdom.

As Thea entered her father was standing with his back to the mantelpiece.

"Good evening, my dear!" he said. "I have been very busy all day, but now I want to talk to you."

Thea kissed his cheek and sat down on the sofa.

She clasped her hands tightly together, aware of what was coming.

"You are now eighteen," the King began, "and we have to think about your future."

"I am very happy as I am, Papa."

"I am very happy to have you with me," the King said. "As the same time your mother was only eighteen when we were married."

Thea was just about to say; "To a man only five years older than herself."

Then she realised to do so would be to betray Georgi's confidence, and her father would know he had already told her about King Otho.

"I have been thinking who would best help our beloved country," the King went on, "if they had a close alliance with us."

He paused as if he expected Thea to speak and when she did not do so he went on:

"As it happens, I had a letter this morning from King Otho, asking if he might come here in four days time."

Thea drew in her breath.

She clenched her fingers until the knuckles were white.

"I have the idea," her father went on, "that he had almost clairvoyantly realised what I have been thinking."

"What . . is that . . Papa?" Thea asked.

Her voice did not sound like her own.

"An alliance between Otho's country and ours would be very advantageous for us."

He glanced at his daughter before he added:

"I have therefore sent a reply to tell him how warmly he will be welcomed, and how much we look forward to his visit."

"Are you . . saying, Papa," Thea asked, "that you think . . King Otho would . . make me a . . suitable husband?"

"You would be Queen of a large and prosperous country and in that position I am sure you could help Kostas in a thousand different ways."

Thea drew in her breath.

"I . . I am sorry, Papa . . but I . . cannot marry King Otho!"

"What did you say?" her father asked.

"H . . he is . . old . . much too old for me!" Thea said. "And . . if I do marry . . I wish to be . . in love!"

"What do you mean – if you *do* marry?" the King

asked. "Of course you have to marry! It is your duty to do so!"

"But not to a man who is . . old enough to be . . my father!"

"Old? What has age to do with it?" the King demanded. "He is a King, and you will be a Queen!"

His voice was sharp, but Thea replied:

"I want to . . love the man I . . marry!"

"Love? Love?" the King said. "That is all young women think about. Well, there is every reason to think you will grow to love your husband."

"How can you be . . sure of . . that?" Thea asked.

With an effort the King tried to be conciliatory.

"You are very young, my dear," he said, "and you must therefore allow me to know what is best for you. I feel sure that Otho will always be kind and treat you with propriety."

"But . . I want to be . . loved!" Thea persisted.

"Love will come after marriage," the King answered firmly.

"How can you be sure?" Thea demanded. "If I do not find him attractive now, why should he be any different just because I have his ring on my finger?"

Her father hesitated and she knew he was finding it difficult to explain in words what he was thinking.

There was quite a long silence. Then Thea rose to her feet.

"I am sorry, Papa, but I will not . . marry King Otho and . . it would . . therefore be a . . mistake to let him come . . here under . . false pretences."

The King glared at her.

"Are you teaching me how to behave?" he demanded angrily. "Good God, most girls would be thrilled at the prospect of becoming a reigning Queen!"

"Not with a man as old as King Otho!" Thea retorted.

"What does it matter is he is old or young?" the King shouted.

"It matters to me! *I* have to marry him – not you!"

The King lost his temper.

"How dare you speak to me like that?" he roared. "You will do as you are told, and I will have no nonsense about it!"

"What will you do?" Thea asked. "Drag me to the altar unconscious? I swear I will not say the words which will make me his wife!"

Her father went crimson in the face.

"Dammit!" he shouted. "You are enough to try the patience of a Saint! You will do as you are told, Thea, and that is my last word on the subject!"

He looked at his daughter as he spoke and realised she was still defying him.

She was small and fragile-looking. Yet at the moment there was a strange resemblance between them.

They were both completely determined to have their own way.

"You will marry the King!"

The words from her father's lips seemed to echo round the room.

"I will not . . Papa! I completely . . refuse!"

"Very well," the King said, "unless you change your mind within the next twenty-four hours, you will be confined to your room, and will have nothing to eat but bread and water."

Thea glared back at him as he went on:

"You will not be allowed to ride and your horse Mercury will be sold at the Horse Fair which takes place in two days time!"

The blood seemed to drain away from Thea's face.

"Did you . . say," she asked, "that you would . . sell Mercury?"

"I am a man of my word," the King said. "Unless you consent to marry King Otho, Mercury will be sold."

For a moment Thea just stood staring at him.

Then with a cry of a small animal caught in a trap, she turned and ran from the room.

Thea ran upstairs and went into her bedroom. She closed the door and locked it.

Then as she threw herself down on the bed she burst into tears.

She cried helplessly, knowing that her father had won.

She loved Mercury who had been hers ever since he was born.

She loved him in many ways more than she loved her own family.

He was a part of her, he belonged to her, and it was impossible, she thought, to live without him.

For a moment she actively hated her father.

He was using the one weapon which he knew would render her powerless to defy him.

She thought helplessly that she would marry the Devil himself rather than think of Mercury belonging to anybody else.

He might be ill-treated, starved or beaten and she would be unable to prevent it.

He would not understand, he would not know what had happened to him.

"I shall have to marry King Otho!"

She felt as if a Demon was bending over her.

He was forcing her to humiliate herself by accepting her father's decision.

She lay crying on her bed until there was a knock on the door.

"What is it?" she asked.

"It's Martha, Your Royal Highness. It's time you dressed for dinner."

"I am too ill to go down to dinner!" Thea replied.

"Very well, Your Royal Highness, I'll tell them to send your dinner upstairs."

Martha went away.

It was a question, Thea thought, of whether she was given what everybody else was having, or bread and water.

She knew that her father would be aware that he had won the battle.

He had conquered her.

She was obliged, like a slave at his chariot-wheel, to obey his orders.

She would marry King Otho and it would be a grand wedding.

Everybody in the City would throng the streets, cheering, waving and showering her with rose-petals.

Waiting in the Cathedral would be an old, white-haired man.

He had buried his first wife and was marrying again, Thea was sure, simply because he wanted an heir.

It was then that she felt herself shudder.

It was with a repugnance that was greater than anything she had felt before.

She had no idea what happened when a man and a woman made love to each other.

She knew of course, that when people were married they slept in the same bed.

King Otho would sleep beside her, he would touch her with his old, blue-veined hands.

She supposed he would kiss her.

She felt herself scream at the thought of his thin lips touching hers.

"I cannot bear it . . I cannot!"

The tears were running down her cheeks.

Then she was thinking again of Mercury.

Thinking how well he had taken the jumps this morning.

How he always nuzzled against her when she went to the stables.

How he would come when she called him.

Mercury! Mercury? How could she bear to lose him?

She walked to the window and stood looking out.

Now because it was still Spring, the sun had already sunk and the sky was crimson and gold on the horizon.

The last rays from the sun lingered on the snow on the mountain peaks and high overhead the first evening star twinkled in the sky.

It was so beautiful that despite her misery Thea felt it lifted her heart.

On earth life might be horrifying, degrading and revolting.

High above her was Heaven if only she could reach it.

She thought of how Apollo had driven his magnificent horses across the sky.

He brought light to those who were in darkness.

It was the light which lifted not only their hearts, but also their minds.

She pictured herself riding in the same way across the sky on Mercury.

Then as she visualised herself galloping into the crimson and gold as it sank lower and lower, she had an idea.

An idea so stupendous, so revolutionary, that she could for a moment, hardly grasp it.

With a cry she flung up her arms as she was reaching out to the stars overhead.

They had given her an answer, brought the light to her mind.

"I will do it!" she cried. "That is what I will do!"

Chapter Two

Thea lay in the darkness thinking out her plan in detail.

She would take Mercury and disappear until after King Otho had left.

Her father would be furiously angry but it would take time to set up another State Visit.

She was well aware that a visiting Monarch from another country expected an enormous amount of kow-towing, special Banquets and Receptions.

She had always found them incredibly dull.

Such occasions however delighted her father and gave him a chance to show off what Kostas could do.

As soon as dinner was finished, he would go to his Study to make plans first for the Reception for King Otho at the frontier.

Then there would be a series of what Thea thought of as 'Charades' to impress him.

The Army, such as it was, would be on parade, and canons would be fired.

Everything would lead up to the moment when her engagement would be announced.

"I will . . not do . . it! I will . . not!" she said to give herself courage.

She knew she was being outrageous and revolutionary.

Her father would be appalled by her behaviour.

It would however, she thought, give him a sharp and salutary jolt to realise that she had a will of her own.

At the same time, she felt for the moment helpless.

If she rode away, where could she go, and what was more important than anything else, she had no money.

She thought about this for some time, then got out of bed and went to the window to look up at the stars.

"You have to help me," she said, "you must guide me."

She remembered how a star had guided the Three Wise Men on their way to Bethlehem. That was what she needed now.

Almost as if in answer to her prayer, she recalled something she had forgotten.

She had no ready money because she never needed it.

If she went shopping the bills were always sent to the Palace.

If she wished to purchase something in the Market Place or to give a few small coins to a beggar, it was supplied by her Lady-in-Waiting.

She invariably accompanied her on such occasions.

It had never struck her until now that she was penniless, and it was in fact, an uncomfortable feeling.

Then she was sure it was the stars that reminded her that she did have some money.

Ever since her birth, one of her Godfathers, an Archduke, gave her a present every Christmas, of a golden coin of the highest denomination in Kostas.

Each bore the date of the year in which he presented it.

She therefore had eighteen such gold coins.

They constituted a sum of money which would pay for everything she needed a dozen times over.

She thought therefore, she would take ten of them from where she kept her special treasures.

That was the cabinet in her Sitting-Room.

Besides the gold coins there was a very pretty snuffbox which Georgi had bought her as a present, the last time he was in Paris.

There was a necklace made of sea-shells.

She had strung them together years ago when she had been taken for a holiday by the sea.

There was also a necklace made of cherry stones which she had been given by one of the Gypsies.

The Gypsies passed through Kostas usually in the Summer.

Because her father was a kindly man, unlike some of the other reigning Monarchs, he welcomed them.

They had always fascinated Thea.

She often went and talked to them and they taught her a little of their Romany tongue.

One of the young girls had shown her once a necklace of cherry stones.

"This, Your Royal Highness," she said, "is magic."

"In what way?" Thea asked.

"When a gypsy girl sees a man she wants to fall in love with her," the Gypsy answered, "she collects as many cherry stones as the years of her age. She drills a hole through one stone each night beginning with the night of the New Moon."

"What happens then?" Thea enquired.

"She continues for three full moons, then she sleeps for thirteen nights with the necklace wound around her left knee."

Thea was listening intently to the Gypsy who went on:

"When the necklace has won her a proposal of marriage from the man she loves, she keeps it for the rest of her life."

She looked at Thea as she said:

"I won the man whom I loved and he loves me. You keep this necklace, Your Royal Highness, and it will show you how to make magic when you need it."

Thea thanked her and she had taken the necklace home and put it in her glass cabinet.

Now she took it out and held it in her hands.

"Help me to find a man I can love and who will love me," she prayed.

Then she put it back in the case.

She picked out ten of the golden coins and put them in her pocket.

She was certain that ten of the most recent years would be easy to replace, the eight earlier ones which bore her grandfather's head might be more difficult.

Anyway she now had money, and that was essential.

She went back into her bedroom and packed what she intended to take with her.

She would have to carry everything in a roll attached to the back of Mercury's saddle.

It would therefore have to be light.

She chose one of the muslin gowns and thought she would change in the evenings.

She added a clean white blouse, a nightgown and a few small things that were indispensable.

She packed it all in a woollen shawl which would be warm enough to cover her shoulders if she was cold, and it would also have to act as a dressing-gown.

A pair of satin slippers would, she knew, go into the pocket of the saddle, with her hair-brush and comb.

Then there was a small bag containing her soap, her tooth-brush, a sponge and a flannel.

She wrapped it all in a chiffon scarf.

She tried to think if there was anything else she required.

Then leaving everything ready on a chair she got into bed.

She did not expect to sleep.

But she was tired and slept dreamlessly almost as soon as her head touched the pillow.

*

Thea awoke with a start.

It flashed through her mind that she had over-slept and it would spoil her plan of escape.

Then she remembered she had been looking at the stars when she had got into bed and had left the curtains drawn back.

It was dawn that had awakened her.

The first pale fingers of light were creeping up the sky.

For the moment the stars were still shining brightly overhead.

Then Thea knew they would soon begin to fade.

Before they did so she wished to be on her way.

She glanced at the clock and saw it was just after four in the morning.

It took her only a few minutes to dress. She had put on one of her prettiest habits which matched the green of her eyes.

Her mother refused to be interested in the new, tight-fitting riding habits which had just come into fashion, having been introduced by Elizabeth, the Empress of Austria, who was also Queen of Hungary.

Thea's habit was very becoming.

It had a full skirt and she wore with it a thin muslin blouse under a tight-fitting jacket.

Under her skirt were two white petticoats edged with lace.

Her riding boots reached only to her ankles.

With the habit went a riding-hat that had a high crown and encircled with a gauze veil which floated out behind her when she galloped.

This morning however Thea was not interested in her appearance.

She dressed quickly.

Sweeping her long hair round her head she fixed it in place with hair-pins.

She looked at her hat, then decided not to take it with her.

When she rode alone in the Park she always went hatless.

Occasionally her mother would say:

"Do be careful, dearest, of the sun. It would be very unbecoming if you had brown skin with your coloured hair."

Thea was fortunate.

The Fairies at her Christening had given her a white skin that was impervious to the sun.

"Your skin is like magnolia!" somebody had said to her once, and she knew that was the truth.

There was also something translucent about it, which made her glow like a pearl.

However there was nobody in the Palace who would dare to compliment her.

In consequence she had no idea how lovely she looked.

Because she was excited, her eyes were shining and she typified the joy of Spring.

She put a clean handkerchief into her pocket, and remembered to pack two more in her luggage.

Pausing for a moment, she wondered if she should write a letter to her father. Then she decided it would be a mistake.

It would be best for her to just disappear. That she had done so would gradually percolate through the Palace.

When Martha found she was not in her bedroom she would assume that she had gone riding.

When she did not come back for breakfast, she doubted if anyone would notice.

Her father was used to her being late and it was the only meal at which the servants did not wait.

They would think she had come and gone.

Much later in the morning, her mother, who always rose late, might be told that she was not in the Palace.

The Queen would not be perturbed, thinking as usual she was riding.

It might easily be luncheontime before anyone would seriously question her whereabouts.

'And by that time,' Thea thought with satisfaction, 'I shall be miles and miles away!'

Holding her two bundles she peeped out through the door into the passage. There appeared to be no one about.

On tip-toe she hurried to a staircase which led to the door into the garden.

It was the one that she and Georgi always used when they had no wish to be seen or encounter either of their parents.

If they did they were likely to be given a task they did not want.

Thea reached the garden-door and unlocked it.

As she stepped out the air was fresh, clean and fragrant with the scent of flowers. She slipped through the garden like a ghost.

When she reached the stables there was a groom on duty. He was a young lad and was asleep on a bundle of hay.

Thea woke him by touching his arm.

"Sorry, Ye Royal Highness, I just dozed off!"

"That is all right," Thea smiled. "I am early because I could not sleep. Please saddle Mercury for me."

"Right ye are, Your Royal Highness," the boy said and hurried to where Mercury was stabled.

As soon as the horse saw Thea he nuzzled her and she made a fuss of him all the time he was being saddled.

The stable-boy led him out into the yard and Thea climbed onto the mounting-block.

She had trained Mercury to stand steady while she seated herself in the saddle.

As she did so she said to the boy as he handed her the reins:

"Will you fix this onto Mercury's saddle?"

She gave him her shawl and he attached the ribbons with which she had bound it to the saddle-loops.

Thea quickly put the other small bundle into the pocket of the saddle.

She knew the boy would not think it strange that she should carry something at the back.

If it rained or was cold she often took a coat with her.

He was not very intelligent, but he might however think it unusual that she was taking so much with her.

She waited until the boy had finished. Mercury showed his impatience by twitching his ears and tossing his head.

Then when the boy had finished Thea said:

"Thank you very much."

"'Ave a nice ride, Ye Royal Highness!" the boy replied, and touched his forelock.

She rode off, deliberately not hurrying.

Only when she was in the Park and out of sight of the Palace did she make Mercury move quickly.

There was only one way she could leave the Palace grounds without passing through a gate that was guarded by sentries.

All the main entrances had soldiers on duty.

Although Thea suspected they did not exert themselves unduly at any of them.

There was however one very minor gate which was used only by farm-carts and the animals which came in to graze from the Home Farm.

Because it was of no importance there was nobody on guard.

Although it was supposed to be locked at night, Thea doubted if this always happened.

She however, had no intention of dismounting to find out.

The gate was quite a low one and the ground around it dry and sandy.

Mercury cleared it with at least a foot to spare.

Now Thea was outside the Royal fence which had hedged her in ever since she could remember.

She had often ridden down to the valley but had never been allowed to do so alone.

If nothing else, she thought, this was a new experience.

She settled down to ride quickly but carefully, as she must not encounter anyone who would recognise her.

This meant she had to be far away from the Palace before it was light.

The dawn was forcing back the sable of the sky. The stars were fading one by one and soon it would be light.

What she had to do was to cross the river before other people were doing the same.

She knew numbers of peasants came in early from the country to Gyula, the Capital of Kostas.

Some of them would be in carts loaded with vegetables for the market.

Others would be carrying what they had to sell on their backs.

Then there would be the women who came in from the country every day to work.

Thea had often seen them and thought how colourful they looked.

They were in National costume which as in all the Balkan countries had traditionally a red skirt, a prettily embroidered blouse and a black velvet corset which was laced down the front.

The Kostasians were a happy people. They would be laughing and singing as they walked along the road.

When they saw either Thea or Georgi they would wave excitedly and call out greetings in their musical voices.

Thea reached the bridge.

She found to her relief that there was no-one on it.

It was also too early for anyone to be working in the fields.

Or to be driving their animals over the open land beyond which stretched the foot of the mountains.

That was for the moment her main objective.

It was very like the Steppes of Hungary, covered with thick grass filled with wild flowers.

It was a perfect place for Mercury to stretch his legs in a wild gallop.

He did not have to be told what to do. Thea thought she had never moved so quickly.

By the time she had ridden a mile or two the sun had risen over the horizon and its rays, warm and golden, lit the world.

The butterflies, white and colourful, were hovering over the flowers. The birds were singing, and the mist had risen from the river.

To Thea it was all the beauty she sought.

The beauty that was in her dreams.

She did not know where she was going.

She thought last night the stars had told her to escape and now she would be guided by the sun.

"I am . . free! I am . . free!" she told herself.

Mercury slowed down from a gallop to an easy trot.

She looked back.

She had come even further than she had expected.

There was no sign of Gyula and nothing to be seen of the Palace which rose higher than the City.

"I am free!" she said again and wondered where she should go.

She rode on until she realised that she was in a part of the country where she had never been before.

Now there was no sign of the river, nor were there any cultivated fields.

There were just the flowers, the butterflies and to her right and ahead the mountains.

She knew however there were many passes through them, some were regularly utilised and some were not.

She had never had a chance to explore them.

When she went riding outside the Palace grounds, either with her father or Georgi, there always had come the moment when they said:

"We should be going back or we will be late for luncheon."

Then again, if they rode in the afternoon, they had to return in plenty of time for dinner which was always a formal meal.

Thea rode on for an hour or so before she thought she was feeling hungry.

She remembered that later in the day she would have to find somewhere to stay the night.

She knew there were small lodging houses or hotels where visitors to Kostas stayed, especially those who enjoyed climbing.

It was something Georgi had attempted and only gave it up after he had fallen and broken his arm.

There were also sportsmen who came to Kostas to shoot the chamois, other stalked the stags, the wild goats and the wolves.

Her father always talked about them rather scathingly.

There were woven fur-rugs and stag horns in the Palace which proclaimed his prowess when he was younger.

"There must be a small hotel near here," Thea told herself.

For the moment there was no hurry and she drew a little nearer to the mountains.

Then she saw a pass rising higher than the land on which she was riding. There was a rough track leading up to it.

Because she thought it would be a good place to hide she rode Mercury up the track.

38

Nearer the top, with the rocks rising on either side of her, she turned to look back.

She realised she had come a very long way.

If her father sent soldiers to look for her it would take days for them to search in the mountains.

She rode on up the pass which could only be negotiated on a horse or on foot, but it was narrow and not very long.

As it ended she found herself in a forest of fir trees.

The trees were thick so that the sunshine could hardly percolate through them.

Thea loved the woods, feeling they were mysterious and filled with dragons and elves.

She had read about Sylvanus, God of the Trees, and had often thought of him when she rose in the wood behind the Palace.

But that was very different from the trees through which she was riding now which were thick dark fir-trees, very tall because they reached towards the light.

They were mysterious and, Thea thought, definitely part of her Fairy-Story.

Suddenly there was an opening and she saw to her surprise a small lake with trees lining each side of it.

The sunshine glittered dazzlingly on the water.

She was entranced because as she drew Mercury to a halt she could see the snow-topped mountains above her.

At the same time she saw a profusion of yellow irises growing on the sides of the lake.

It was so lovely she would not have been surprised if she had seen a water-nymph.

She was sure Mercury was thirsty, so she rode him down to the water's edge then dismounted.

Before she did so she knotted his reins then leaving him to drink as much as he wanted she walked on, looking at the lake, the flowers and the trees.

She felt as if she had stumbled into a strange world.

Everything was different from anything she had ever seen before.

She was so intent on what she was seeing that she was not looking ahead and suddenly she realised she had almost fallen over a man who was sitting on a low stool.

In front of him was an easel on which stood a canvas.

He was obviously painting the lake and concentrated intently on his work so he was not aware of her presence.

She glanced at his canvas and thought that as a painter he was obviously talented. At the same time he was the first person she had seen since leaving the Palace.

She hoped he would be able to tell her what she wished to know.

"Excuse me, *Mein Herr*," she began politely, "can you tell me where . . . ?"

Before she could finish the sentence the Artist exclaimed:

"Go away! Leave me alone! I am busy!"

He spoke so angrily that Thea was astonished.

Apart from her father, nobody had ever spoken to her in such a way.

For a moment she did not move.

Then, as if he was intending to order her to obey him, the Artist turned his head.

He looked at Thea and was astonished into silence.

He just sat staring at her.

She was looking at him, finding it strange that anybody so rude could be so good-looking. He was unlike any man she had ever seen before.

He had dark hair which was uncovered, straight, classical features, and what she thought were almost black eyes.

There seemed to be a long silence before he said:

"I apologise! I was not expecting to be visited by a Goddess from one of the mountains!"

Because she could not help it, Thea laughed.

She had always believed there were gods and goddesses living on top of the snow-capped mountains.

They would show their disapproval by sending down cascades of icy water or would reward those they favoured with an abundance of wild strawberries.

As he went on looking at Thea, the Artist rose to his feet.

He was tall, over six foot and his shoulders were broad.

She realised that he showed his profession by the way he was dressed.

He had discarded his coat because the sun was warm, especially as the lake was sheltered by trees.

He was wearing instead of a tie, a red silk scarf round his neck which was tied in a large bow.

As Thea did not speak the Artist said:

"Please forgive me, and let me try to answer the question I did not allow you to finish."

He seemed so contrite that Thea smiled and said:

"Perhaps it is I who should apologise for interrupting you when you were painting anything so beautiful."

"I was cross because I could not capture it," the Artist said. "How can I depict the dancing light on the water, and the mystery of the trees?"

Thea stared at him in astonishment.

It was what she thought herself, but nobody else had ever said it to her before.

"May I look at your picture?" she asked.

The Artist spread out his hands.

"I am honoured you should do so," he said. "At the same time, I am well aware that I am an inadequate painter."

Thea moved closer to the easel.

She saw at first glance that the painting was very different from any of the pictures hanging in the Palace.

It was not a precise representation of the lake or the trees.

It was, she thought, an impression and yet in some strange way he had captured the magic that more traditional artists would not have been able to do.

She was looking at it, unaware that the Artist was watching her.

At length she said:

"I think you are painting what you feel rather than what you see. It is clever! I can feel the goblins under the trees, and the nymphs beneath the water!'

She was speaking to herself rather than to him, then as he did not reply she turned to look at him.

"You *are* a goddess from the mountains!" he said. "No one else has ever understood what I am trying to do."

'It is . . difficult to put into . . words."

"Of course," he answered, "but what you are thinking is much more important."

Thea was going to ask him how he could speak like that when Mercury came to join her.

At the sound the Artist turned his head to look with even more astonishment at the huge black stallion with just a white star on his forehead.

"So this is how you reached me!" he said.

"This is Mercury!" Thea said by way of introduction.

"The Messenger of the Gods!" the Artist exclaimed. "How could he be anything else?"

He patted Mercury on the neck and Thea said:

"What I was going to ask you was if you knew of anywhere near here where Mercury and I could have . . something to eat. We have . . travelled a . . long way."

"I can understand that," the Artist said glancing up at the mountain peaks directly above them, "but I am afraid I cannot offer you Ambrosia!"

"I will accept . . anything that is . . edible!" Thea smiled.

As she thought about it she was indeed feeling hungry, having eaten nothing since last night.

Even then because her father had upset her, she had only picked at the food that Martha had brought to her.

She had been thinking all the time of having to marry King Otho and the food had therefore seemed to stick in her throat.

The Artist closed his paint-box and put his canvas under his arm.

He left both the easel and the stool where they were, making it clear that he intended to come back later.

Thea thought that he was not taking the risk of losing his picture although she doubted if there was anybody in the vicinity who was likely to steal it.

Then as an afterthought he asked:

"Do you wish to ride, or will you walk? It is not very far."

"I will walk," Thea answered.

They moved along a track which wound through the wood and Mecury followed them.

"I feel rather guilty," Thea said conversationally, "for taking you away from your work. You could have told me where I could go."

"Apart from the fact that it would be very impolite," the Artist replied, "I have just realised that I am hungry."

Thea laughed.

"I feel the same, but I was so enjoying my ride that I forgot everything else."

"Are you really riding alone?" the Artist enquired.

"Yes."

The one syllable told him better than more words that she did not wish to speak about it.

He glanced at her profile because she was looking away from him. There was a twinkle in his eyes, but he did not say any more.

They walked in silence until the trees suddenly came to an end, and there, just in front of them was a small building.

It was perched on the side of a mountain with a cliff below it which fell hundreds of feet down into a valley.

Thea looked in astonishment.

It was a very different valley from the one she had just left.

To begin with, there were many more woods and it all seemed wild and uncultivated, but at the same time very beautiful.

There were no mountains straight ahead.

The land seemed to go on into infinity.

She realised that this was another country, and she had left her own.

But for the moment she did not want to ask any questions.

She was so afraid she would find that she was in Guhen and that was King Otho's Kingdom.

The Artist was leading her towards the house.

As they got nearer to it, Thea thought it was a very strange place to find an Hotel.

As far as she could see, either beyond or below it, there was no other building.

She was just about to ask the Artist for an explanation when a young man came hurrying towards him.

"I just coming, Master," he said, "to tell you time for luncheon."

"Tell your mother I have a guest for luncheon," the Artist said, "and tell Valou there is a hungry horse that requires a stable."

The boy looked at Mercury.

Then he ran to do the Artist's bidding.

Thea was aware that both the Artist and the boy had spoken in a langauge that was different from the language of Kostas.

She could understand what he was saying.

She knew that she had learnt his language, but for the moment she could not put a name to it.

44

They had gone only a short distance before an older man appeared.

Thea thought he would be recognisable anywhere as being connected with horses.

He gave an exclamation when he saw Mercury, and she knew it was one of admiration.

"Give him a good meal, Valou," the Artist said, "which is what I intend to have myself."

The groom bowed politely to Thea as he passed her.

He patted Mercury before he took him by the bridle.

When the horse went with him without making a fuss, Thea knew he was experienced with animals.

"We go this way," the Artist said.

She saw he was taking her to the front of the small house.

There was a balcony outside and she saw there was a table already laid for one with a white table-cloth.

It had an orange coloured umbrella above it to keep off the sun.

The Artist however walked in through the door that led into the hall. Thea following found it was very different from what she had expected.

The hall was small and painted white.

The only decoration consisted of several paintings like the one the Artist had been doing by the lake.

At a glance she could see that all had the same characteristics that made her know he was painting what he felt.

"If you go upstairs," he said, "you will find a room on the left where I am sure you would like to wash your hands."

"Thank you," Thea replied.

She went up the stairs thinking this was indeed an unexpected adventure.

She found the room which was not difficult, as there were only two doors at the top of the stairs; one to the right, and one to the left.

The room to which she had been directed was as surprising as the hall.

It was small but the window had a view over the valley which was breathtaking.

Most of the room seemed to be filled with a very large bed.

It was distinctive because the back, the sides and the feet were all carved and painted.

Thea knew it was the work of local craftsmen but the workmanship was far superior to anything she had seen before.

The headboard depicted flowers that she had seen by the lake, a great number which she knew were wild.

Amongst them nestled birds, most of which she knew by name.

There were one or two however that were strangers.

Their brilliant plumage, the colours of the flowers, and the skilful manner in which they had been massed together was lovely.

For a moment she could only stand staring at it.

Then she realised that the bed cover was also the product of local talent.

There were many women in Kostas who made lace with their bobbins. What she was looking at now was outstanding work, and very lovely.

On the polished wooden floor there were white rugs of chamois skin.

She washed her hands in a china bowl which she was certain was the work of local potters.

It was all so fascinating.

She admired it for some time before she looked for a mirror which again was carved very delicately and was surmounted by two fat little cupids which had been coloured in natural hues.

She tidied her hair which had been swept into curls by the wild way in which she had galloped on Mercury.

Then she went downstairs.

The Artist was waiting for her on the balcony outside.

She was sure it was a concession that he had put on a coat of some light material and a different scarf at his neck, this time it was blue.

It too was tied in a bow in the front.

She wondered if he wore the velvet tam-o'-shanter adopted by French artists.

She had however no wish to ask any uncomfortable questions or to appear critical.

She saw as she joined her host that another chair had been placed beside the table.

She sat down under the shade of the orange umbrella, the sun was high in the sky, and it was very hot.

As if he read her thoughts, the Artist said:

"Why do you not take off your riding-coat?"

"What a good idea!" Thea agreed.

He helped her out of her coat and as he put it down she looked at the view and said:

"I think I am dreaming! I had no idea anything could be so lovely!"

"Nor had I!" the Artist replied, but he was looking at her.

He poured something from a jug into her glass, and when she looked at it, he explained:

"It is a fruit juice which is a speciality. I hope you enjoy it."

She lifted it to her lips and found it delicious.

Then, because she was curious, she had to ask:

"Is this your house? Do you live here?"

"It is my house," he replied.

"How could you have found anything so different – so unusual?" Thea asked.

"I must have known instinctively that one day it would be what you wanted," he replied.

She laughed.

"That is a pretty speech, but I think it was very clever of you to discover anything so unique!"

"I thought that myself," he replied.

Once again he was looking at her.

It flashed through her mind how shocked her father and mother would be that she was alone with a very handsome young man in a house where there was no chaperon.

The boy who had met them brought out the first dish.

Now as he came towards them he was not in his shirt-sleeves.

He had put on a clean white jacket, and he had brushed his hair.

"I usually have a small luncheon," the Artist was saying, "but I promise to provide you with something more exotic at dinner."

Thea's eyes opened wide.

"Dinner?" she exclaimed. "But I was . . not planning to . . stay."

"Where are you going?"

She realised she had no answer to this and after a moment she said:

"I . . I am not quite . . certain but . . further on."

"Why?"

There really seemed to be no answer to that.

She had to be as far as possible from the Palace, but that was something she could not say.

They were eating a salad of eggs, fish, lettuce and tomatoes.

Because she was hungry, Thea thought that every mouthful was a joy.

It was followed by a dish of young, tender chicken cooked with cream and it was flavoured with herbs that Thea did not recognise.

There were tiny potatoes, so small it seemed cruel to

eat them, peas that were also minute and little carrots no bigger than Thea's smallest finger.

After this there was cheese, several different varieties.

Coffee, black and fragrant, completed one of the most delicious meals Thea had ever enjoyed.

They did not talk much while they were eating and when they had finished the Artist sat back in his chair.

"Now tell me about yourself," he said. "First of all, I do not know your name."

"It is Thea."

She knew as she spoke she was quite safe in saying that, for only her family called her Thea.

To the people of Kostas she was Princess Sydel.

"But I do not know your name," she said, "and I cannot go on thinking of you as 'The Artist'!"

He laughed.

"That is a compliment, but I am too conscious of my short-comings to be entitled to it!"

"Of course you are entitled to it!" Thea argued. "It is only that I have the idea you are in advance of our time. One day people will understand what you are trying to say."

"How do you know that?" he enquired.

Thea made a little gesture that explained better than words it was just what she thought.

"Who are you?" he asked. "And where are you going all alone with a horse that could only have come from Olympus."

Thea did not answer and after a moment he said:

"I know without your telling me that you are running away."

She looked at him with startled eyes.

"Why . . should you . . think that?"

"Why should you understand what I am trying to paint?" he retorted.

She decided there was no point in prevaricating.

"Yes . . I am running . . away."

"From a man?"

"Y.yes . . a man!"

That was certainly true and as she thought of King Otho she shuddered.

"Then I can think of no place where you are less likely to be disturbed than here!" the Artist said.

"No . . no . . of course . . not!" Thea replied.

"Why not?"

"Because you are a stranger and . . I do not . . know . . you!"

"My name is Nikōs, and I think we know each other very much better than if we had been introduced formally at a Reception which would have been incredibly dull, except that you were there!"

Because of the way he spoke Thea could not help laughing.

Nikōs bent towards her.

"Why are you running away?"

"Because . . I want . . to be . . free!"

"That is a cry all down the ages, but unfortunately it is impossible."

"Why is it . . impossible?"

"Because you are a woman, and women have to be protected and looked after."

"That is something I have . . no wish to be. I want to be . . myself! I want to . . live my own . . life."

"And to find what you are seeking?" Nikōs said gently.

For a moment she was startled.

Then she told herself he was being uncannily perceptive but he could not know that what she was seeking was love.

The love she was denied because she was a Princess.

Chapter Three

When luncheon was over Nikōs said:

"There are places in the wood I would like to show you. Another day I will take you riding."

Thea looked at him with wide eyes and he said:

"Both you and Mercury have gone far enough today. It would really be cruelty to take him any further."

She opened her lips to say that she could not stay as he suggested.

Then she asked herself 'why not?'

She had to stay somewhere and it suddenly struck her that if she was in an Hotel she might be frightened.

She had not thought of that before, but of course, there might be strange men.

Although Nikōs was what the English would call 'a Gentleman', other men might be rough.

They also might be familiar, she thought, which was something she had never encountered in her whole sheltered life.

She therefore did not answer him directly, and as if he took it for granted that she would do as he suggested, they went into the woods.

Everything, like the thick fir-trees and the forest pools, seemed enchanted.

She was vividly conscious of the mountain peaks high overhead, and wherever there was a clearing in the trees she looked at the overwhelmingly beautiful view.

It was the valley that she had seen from Nikōs's house.

They did not talk much at first.

Yet strangely enough Thea felt as if he understood what she was thinking.

She thought too she could read his thoughts.

Finally they sat down on a mossy bank which sloped down to a small pool in which the water-lilies had first come into flower.

"It is so unbelievably . . lovely that I am sure I am . . dreaming!" Thea explained.

"That is what I have felt ever since I saw you!" Nikōs said.

She felt the colour rise in her cheeks, but she did not look at him and after a moment he said:

"I had forgotten that a woman could blush, or that she could look shy!"

"You must . . not say . . such things . . to me," Thea said in a low voice.

"Why not? I want to tell you how beautiful you are, how intelligent, and . . . "

He hesitated.

Because she was curious, she could not resist glancing at him, hoping he would finish the sentence.

Unexpectedly he said abruptly:

"We should be getting back. The sun is not as warm as it was."

He spoke in a distant voice about a marsh which made Thea feel as if she had suddenly been touched by a cold hand.

Nikōs had risen to his feet.

He was walking slowly back along the twisting path they had followed through the trees.

Suddenly Thea felt frightened, she did not understand!

She got up and ran after him and as she reached his side she asked:

"What . . is the . . matter? What . . have I done . . wrong?"

For a moment she thought he would not reply. Then he said:

"The only thing that is wrong is that you are too beautiful for any man's peace of mind!"

"I . . I cannot help . . my looks."

"What you can help," he said almost angrily, "is wandering about the country on your own. It is something you should not do."

She did not answer and he went on almost as if he spoke to himself.

"I should send you back, otherwise you will get into trouble."

"S.send me . . back? No . . no! I will . . not go!"

Now there was a note of fear in her voice.

"It is something I ought to do," he said.

"But . . why? You have . . no right. It is . . not your . . business!"

He stopped and turned to face her.

"If I leave you to go your own way, what will happen?"

"I was . . thinking about . . that," Thea said, "and . . perhaps it would be . . very frightening."

He did not say anything, and she looked up at him.

"Please . . let me . . stay with . . you," she asked pleadingly.

"Is that what you want?"

"I was . . thinking it could be . . very difficult for me in an . . Hotel."

"Very difficult indeed!" he agreed.

"I . . I did not . . think of that when I . . ran away."

She saw by the expressions on his face what Nikōs was thinking.

"Let me stay . . please . . let me stay," she begged, "at least for . . tonight."

He smiled.

"As you have come for many miles, I really have no choice."

"I will be no . . trouble . . and if you want . . I will . . leave in the . . morning."

"We will discuss that when the morning comes."

She knew she could stay, and she felt an overwhelming relief.

"Thank you," she said. "Thank you . . very . . much!"

"I think I must add a condition to my invitation," Nikōs said.

"What is . . it?" Thea asked nervously.

"That you tell me why you have run away and from whom!"

She stiffened.

"I . . I do not want . . to tell anyone . . and it is a . . secret!"

She sounded agitated, so he capitulated.

"Very well," he said, "keep your secrets, and as you told me you want to be free, let us just enjoy ourselves."

Thea's eyes lit up.

"That would be . . lovely! And when we . . get back to the . . house I want to see . . Mercury."

"Of course!" Nikōs said. "But I assure you he is very comfortable. Valou will see to that!"

They walked on a little way. Then Nikōs asked:

"How can you have acquired such a remarkably outstanding horse?"

'I have had him since a foal, and I love him more than anyone else in the whole world!"

Nikōs raised his eye-brows.

"That is very sweeping!"

"It is true! I am happiest when I am with Mercury, and he understand when I talk to him like . . . "

She stopped feeling what she had been about to say was too intimate.

". . . like I do!" Nikōs said softly.

"I . . I did not say . . that!"

"But that is what you were thinking."

"Now you are . . reading my . . thoughts . . and it is . . something you must . . not do!"

"It is too late for you to stop me from doing something that has happened amazingly since you first appeared."

Thea walked on a little way before she said:

"It is very strange . . but no one . . before has ever . . understood what I was thinking . . and what I . . tried to express . . in my . . music."

"I might have guessed you were musical," Nikōs said.

"Why?"

"Because everything about you is a poem, your looks, the way you walk, your voice."

Thea looked at him with her green eyes.

"That is a lovely thing to tell me; and something I will always remember."

"I have always been told that the women of Kostas have musical voices," Nikōs said, "but yours is like the song of the birds."

Thea made a little murmur and he went on:

"I know without your telling me that there is Hungarian blood in you."

"My grandmother was Hungarian!"

"And so was mine!" Nikōs said. "That is another bond we have in common!"

Thea laughed.

"And I am sure you ride like a Hungarian!"

"As you do!"

The little house was in sight and now the sun was sinking low over the plain.

It turned everything to gold and made the world so beautiful that Thea drew in her breath.

"Shall I try to paint it for you?" Nikōs asked softly.

"That is what I would . . like you to . . do."

Then with a little start she said:

"You are reading my . . thoughts again!"

"Your eyes are very revealing, but I feel that it would be impossible to depict them on canvas."

"I am glad about that! I hate being painted!"

She thought of the long sittings she had had to endure because some organisations in Gyula were always asking for a portrait of her.

She was hung in the Schools, in the Council Chamber, and she thought how different those portraits were from the paintings done by Nikōs.

Sitting stiffly in white satin with a curtain draped behind her, her hands in her lap, she looked very unlike herself.

"I will paint you against the trees, with your face reflected in the lake where we met," Nikōs said.

Thea smiled, but before she could say that was what she would like he went on:

"I will show you as you are – ethereal – half-human and half a 'spirit of the woods'."

He spoke in a low voice, then as if with effort, he said:

"It will soon be dinner-time and Valou's wife will arrange a bath for you in your bedroom."

"That will be lovely!" Thea exclaimed.

She smiled at him and went up the stairs.

As he had told her, there was a bath arranged in the same way as she had it in the Palace.

There was a big can of hot water and another of cold, and the bath was already half-full.

The water in the bath was scented with the fragrance of jasmine.

There were several half-open blossoms floating in it.

As she washed she thought that this was the most exciting adventure she could imagine.

How could she had been so lucky, so incredibly fortunate as to find anyone so interesting as Nikōs?

She thought of the dull, dreary conversations she had with the Courtiers in the Palace.

56

The way Nikōs had talked this afternoon was like the music she played on the piano.

Being with Georgi was always fun, but he was not interested in anything she thought or said, he only wanted her to listen.

He would be happy enjoying himself now in Paris, she thought.

She wished she could see the women who amused him and the Theatres and dances he attended.

Georgi had told her that her mother and father would be shocked at everything he did.

It was difficult for Thea to imagine exactly why.

'Georgi is enjoying himself, and so am I!' she thought defiantly.

By now they would be aware at the Palace that she was missing but she was sure her father would not wish to publicise the matter.

Nor would he want many people to be aware of her disappearance.

She thought it over carefully, she expected he would first of all send Aides-de-Camp to all the places she was likely to be.

She had an old Governess who had retired to a small village about four miles form Gyula.

They would go there and, of course, would call on the Professor.

She thought of the other teachers she had had in the past, and knew it would take time to visit them all.

After that, King Otho would arrive.

Her father would make some excuse for her not being there.

He might say she was ill or staying with relatives. He could hardly tell the King that she had run away because she did not wish to marry him.

As always, when she was thinking of King Otho, she shuddered.

"When he has gone home," she told herself, "I suppose I shall have to go back."

Then she thought she was in no hurry yet but sooner or later she would have to return.

As she got out of the bath she escaped from reality and as always she slipped into one of her Fairy-Stories.

Perhaps she could find a little house like this and live quietly in the country with Mercury.

She would make friends with the peasants with the Gypsies for there were certain to be some in the neighbourhood.

She would need money. She would get the women who had made the lace cover on her bed to teach her how to do it.

It was a simple tale of contentment.

Then once again, as if he was an evil Genie threatening her, she could see King Otho.

He would be waiting for her!

When she was back at the Palace, it would only be a question of whether he came to her or she went to him.

Her father would have pledged his word that she would be his wife.

Because she was so frightened by the idea, Thea dressed hurriedly.

She wanted to go back to Nikōs.

She would talk to him of the woods, the birds, the flowers.

Also of the fairies, elves and water-nymphs in which they both believed.

She put on her muslin gown.

It was a very simple one, made with the material drawn back into classical folds in the front.

The only concession to the fashionable bustle was a sash of the same material. It had silver threads running through it, and ended in a huge bow at the back.

There were frills round the low neck and small puffed sleeves.

It made her look very young, at the same time, there was something very Grecian about her.

When she came down the stairs Nikōs was waiting for her at the bottom.

As she reached him he said:

"Now I know that you have come from the mountain peaks, and are in fact, Divine!"

Thea smiled.

"After that pretty speech it may sound very mundane to say that I am hungry!"

He laughed, and it was a very happy sound.

"No one but you, Thea," he replied, "would say that at this particular moment."

She did not understand what he meant.

He took her into a room she had not seen before because for luncheon they had sat out on the balcony.

It was a very attractive room with a hung window overlooking the valley.

It also had a large fireplace in which there was a big log burning.

She was not surprised, because now the sun had gone down, it could be very cold with icy winds coming from the snow-capped peaks.

The room was warm and although it was white, like the rest of the house, it was also very masculine.

The sofa and chairs were large and comfortable, the floor was covered with fur rugs.

Besides the pictures which had been painted by Nikōs there was a sporting gun and two rifles hanging on the wall.

A magnificent stag's head towered over the fireplace.

Thea looked up at it and said:

"Somehow I cannot imagine you . . shooting in the . . woods!"

"You are quite right! It is something I do not do!"

She looked at he stag's head without asking the obvious question.

"It was given to me by one of the wood-cutters when I first came here," Nikōs explained. "It was his finest possession, and he told me it would bring me luck."

"And has it?"

"What could be luckier than that I should find you?"

Thea smiled.

She had no idea that Nikōs was thinking she was very unlike any other woman.

There was nothing flirtatious in the way she looked at him when he paid her a compliment.

"And the gun?" she questioned.

"It was given to me by a Gypsy I befriended."

He had also been given the rifles. They were elaborately decorated in the style of the beginning of the century.

The gun was also old.

Its butt was carved with miniature animals, each one more exquisite and more life-like than the last.

"Dinner is served, Master!"

It was a boy who had waited on them at luncheon, who spoke from the doorway.

"Thank you, Géza," Nikōs said.

He held out his arm with a mocking smile to Thea.

As she took it she noticed for the first time how he was dressed.

It was in an even more picturesque way than he had been in the daytime.

He wore a white shirt, and over it a black velvet coat which she had expected on an Artist.

Round his waist was a red cummerbund, and the silk scarf round his neck.

On any other man it might have looked affected, but on Nikōs it only added, Thea thought, to his aura of masculinity.

60

She had been conscious of it ever since they met.

He took her into the Dining-Room, which was another room she had not seen before.

It was smaller, and the curtains were drawn over the windows which looked out onto the woods.

They were unlike any curtains she had ever seen.

Only as she looked a little closer did she realise that Nikōs had painted them.

There was an impression of the snow-capped mountains.

Also the flowers she had seen this afternoon, irises and water-lilies, white and blue violets, and wild orchids.

It was quite lovely.

As she was trying to think of words in which to tell Nikōs how clever she thought he was, he said:

"I knew you would appreciate them!"

There was a round table in the centre of the room. It was covered with a lace cloth rather like the cover on her bed.

The Candelabrum in the middle of it which held six candles was of pottery.

Again Thea was certain it was made by local craftsmen.

It showed the stems of flowers entwined together to make the shaft of the Candelabrum and the candles sat in the open petals of the flowers.

Géza brought in the food, which was as unusual as it was delicious.

There were small river crabs cooked in a way Thea had never met before.

There were partridges prepared in red wine which seemed to melt in the mouth, and cutlets of tiny baby lamb.

To finish they had tiny strawberries which must have just ripened in the sun.

Nikōs insisted that she should drink the 'wine of the country.'

As she sipped it, Thea realised she still did not know and she was too afraid it was in King Otho's Kingdom to ask.

When they had finished she said:

"I have never, and this is the truth, had a more delicious dinner!"

"That is what I want you to say," Nikōs smiled, "and Valou's wife will be delighted!"

"If you eat like this every day," Thea said, "I cannot imagine how you remain so slim!"

She had realised when they were walking in the wood that there was something very athletic in the way he moved.

"Tomorrow," he said quietly, "when we ride together, you will realise there is no better exercise!"

"That is what I have always believed," Thea said. "I want to ride and ride every day so that I shall never grow fat!"

Nikōs laughed.

"I am sure that is an impossibility, and I am only afraid that you will fly away from me on the wind."

They went back into the Sitting-Room.

Now the flames were high over the log in the fireplace, the curtains had been drawn and it was very cosy.

Thea sat down, not in a chair, but on the fur rug in front of the fire.

The light on her hair seemed to echo the flames, Nikōs sat looking at her.

Then as the warmth made her yawn he said:

"You are tired."

"I was up very early," she answered.

"How early?"

"Dawn had not yet broken."

"Then you must go to bed."

She did not reply and after a moment he asked:

"Have you enjoyed your first day of freedom?"

"It has been wonderful! More exciting than I can possibly say!"

"What will you do when you have to go back?"

"I have decided I will not go back!"

"Never?"

"Never!" Thea averred firmly.

She thought if she did, however long she had stayed away, she would still be forced to marry King Otho.

She would find some place where her father would never discover her and she would have Mercury with her so that nothing else mattered.

Nikōs did not speak, he was only watching her.

Because Thea thought that he wanted to retire she got to her feet.

"You are right," she said, "I will go to bed. There is always tomorrow, and thank you for being so kind."

He had risen as she had.

Now he stood with his back to the fire looking at her.

"As you say," he said in a deep voice, "there is always tomorrow, and the day after."

She smiled and he went on:

"What matters is that we have found each other!"

As he spoke he put his arms round her and drew her against him.

It was so unexpected that Thea hardly realised what was happening.

Then his lips were on hers.

She was so surprised that she did not struggle.

She only knew she had not realised that a kiss could hold her completely captive, so that she felt it was impossible to move.

Then she felt a strange sensation she had never known before streaking through her.

It was like the first notes of a Sonata.

Only this was music which was playing in her heart.

She felt Nikōs's arms tighten.

His lips became more insistent, demanding and possessive.

She was not frightened.

It was the magic of the fir-trees, the enchantment of the flowers and the shimmering light on the water.

He kissed her until she felt her whole body was pulsating with magic.

She had always known it was there if she could but find it.

Only when he raised his head did she stare at him: her breath was coming quickly from between her parted lips.

"Go to bed, my lovely," he said in a voice that was very deep, and a little hoarse.

It was impossible to speak, because he had carried her up to the mountain peaks.

Thea obeyed him and moving swiftly across the room without looking back she opened the door.

She ran up the stairs into her bedroom.

There was only one candle burning by the side of the bed and her nightgown had been laid out.

The flowers on the headboard seemed a part of the dream-world into which Nikōs had taken her.

She undressed and got into bed.

Only when she was lying back against the pillows could she think and ask herself how it was possible to feel such rapture.

It was different from anything she had ever felt before.

Yet it was familiar because she had known it was there.

She had known it when she played the piano.

Known it when she heard the song of the birds.

She had known it when she looked out over the valley, and when she felt the beauty of it tug at her heart.

She felt as if she was still being carried towards the mountain peaks, to the stars that were shining overhead.

The magic in the woods was whispering a song that she could only sing in her heart.

She was just about to blow out the candle.

Then to her surprise the door opened and Nikōs came in.

He had undressed and was wearing a long robe which was crimson and frogged with gold braid.

He looked different, somehow larger and even more attractive.

He came towards the bed.

As Thea looked at him with wide eyes he sat down on it facing her.

With difficulty, because she had to come back from her dreams, she found her voice.

"W.what do you . . want? Why . . are you . . h.here?"

"I did not finish saying goodnight to you."

"B.but . . I do not . . think you should . . come to my room!"

"Why not."

"It is . . incorrect."

"What we have already done can hardly be called correct!" Nikōs said. "And I think, my darling, you want me a little, as I want you overwhelmingly!"

"I . . I do not . . understand."

"Then let me make it clearer. I will look after you, protect you and hide you, if that is what you want."

"I want that . . but I still do not . . think we need talk about . . it when I am . . in bed."

He looked at her piercingly, until as he realised she really did not understand, he said:

"What I am trying to say, perhaps inadequately, is that I will teach you about love. You will feel even more ecstatic than you felt just now when I kissed you."

"It was . . wonderful!" Thea said, "but I think . . . "

She stopped and gave a little cry.

"Are you.saying that you . . want to . . make love to me?"

"Yes, that is what I want."

"But . . of course you must not do that!"

"Why not?"

"Because . . it is wrong . . very wrong!"

"Why should you think that? How could anything so wonderful be wrong?"

He did not wait for Thea to reply, but bent forward.

For a moment her lips were very soft beneath his.

Then as she excited him so he could no longer go on talking, he put his arms around her.

At the same time he lifted his feet onto the bed.

His lips became fiercer, and Thea felt again the wonder he had given her when he first kissed her.

Then she was aware that his hand was touching her breast and she struggled.

"I want you – God how I want you!" Nikōs said.

"Please . . you must not . . do this!" she gasped.

She did not think he heard her for now he was kissing her neck.

She felt a thrill that was like a streak of forked lightning running through her body.

Then he was pushing the sheet lower.

His hand was moving down her body.

She pressed against his heart and realised how strong he was.

Now she was frightened – really frightened.

"Stop! Please . . stop!" she pleaded.

It was as if Nikōs did not hear.

"I am . . frightened! You are . . frightening . . me! Please . . please . . Nikōs . . listen . . to me! I am . . frightened!"

It was the cry of a child.

It stopped him in a way nothing else would have done.

He raised his head as if he could not believe what he had heard.

He looked down at her.

He saw the terror in her eyes and the tears that were running down her cheeks.

"I am . . frightened!" she said again. "I . . I do not know . . what . . you are . . doing . . but I . . know it is . . wrong!"

The words fell over themselves and her tears blinded her eyes.

He looked at her for a long moment.

Then very slowly he moved off the bed to sit facing her as he had done before.

It was impossible for Thea to stop crying.

At the same time the light from the candle turned her hair to flaming gold.

Her skin was very white and transparent.

She had no idea how utterly desirable she looked.

"Please . . please," she said again incoherently.

Taking a handkerchief from the pocket of his robe, Nikōs bent forward and wiped the tears from her eyes.

"It is all right," he said. "I will not hurt you."

Now he could see the pupils of her eyes were dilated and she was trembling.

"I will not hurt you," he said again. "At the same time, I do not understand."

"You are . . not angry?"

"Only bewildered," he replied. "How can you wander about the countryside alone, talk to a strange man, and stay in his house?"

"You . . asked me to . . stay!"

He smiled.

"Yes, I asked you, and it seemed the obvious thing to do."

He paused before he went on:

"Have you no idea of the dangers you might encounter – in fact, have encountered?"

"I . . I did not . . think of . . that," Thea said hestitatingly.

"You make it very difficult for me, or any other man," Nikōs said.

"Why?"

"You know the answer to that! You are very beautiful and very desirable!"

She looked at him as if she was puzzling out what he meant.

Then she asked.

"Do you mean . . because I look . . pretty it makes . . you want to do . . what is . . wrong?"

"It depends what you mean by wrong," Nikōs said. "I want to make love to you, and I want to make you mine."

She looked at him and she was trembling.

"But I promise you I will not do anything that makes you so frightened," he said quietly, "although it is going to be hard if you stay with me."

"Do you want me to . . go away?"

The fear was back in Thea's voice. Nikōs smiled.

"No, I want you to stay, you know that."

She looked at him uncertainly.

"Perhaps . . I should . . go!"

It flashed through her mind that if she did there were bound to be other men.

They would come to her room as Nikōs had done. They might make love to her whether she tried to stop them or not.

As if he knew what she was thinking he said:

"You can stay here, at least for a little while, but it would be much easier if you did what I wanted."

He thought the fear was back in her eyes and he said gently:

"We will talk about it tomorrow. Go to sleep now, and do not be afraid. The Dragons are all gone!"

"You . . promise you . . are not . . angry with me?"

There was a little twist to his lips as Nikōs replied:

"Shall I say I am disappointed?"

68

He took her hand and raised it to her lips.

"Goodnight, Ice Maiden," he said, "and another time remember to lock your door!"

He got off the bed as he spoke.

"Do you mean . . " Thea asked, "so that you should not . . come in?"

He did not reply, and she said almost beneath her breath:

"I never . . thought of . . it!"

Nikōs had reached the door.

"Forget it, and go to sleep," he said. "As you said earlier, there is always tomorrow."

"And . . you will be . . there?"

"I promise you I will not disappear in the night, but you must promise the same."

Then he went out and shut the door quietly behind him.

She heard him cross the landing and go into the room opposite.

Then there was silence.

She did not blow out the candle instead she lay thinking of what had happened.

Insidiously the rapture she had felt when Nikōs kissed her came back and she felt the wonder of it within her breast.

She could feel too the lightning that had swept through her when he had kissed her neck.

To her horror she found herself wondering why she had stopped him.

Why had she not let him make love to her as he had wanted to?

"It is wrong . . wicked . . and if I had done so . . I would be like the . . women with . . whom Georgi . . enjoys himself . . when he is . . in Paris!"

Yet she wanted Nikōs to kiss her, she wanted him to touch her.

How was it possible she should feel like this for a man she had never seen until this morning?

Yet he had always been in her dreams and in the stories she told herself.

"He was the 'Prince Charming' who would appear unexpectedly, he would love her, as she would love him."

Then she knew that in the Fairy-Tale the Prince asked her to be his wife.

When she said 'yes', they were married and lived happily ever afterwards.

Innocent though she was, Thea knew that Nikōs did not wish to marry her.

He wanted to be her lover.

"It . . would be wrong . . very wrong . . for me to . . agree to anything that was . . so wicked," she told herself.

But her lips were aching for his kisses, and now he had gone she wanted him to stay.

It flashed through her mind that she had only to cross from her room to his and they would be together.

She was shocked at her own feelings, her own thoughts.

She knew then she could not stay.

She got up, took off her nightgown and dressed herself in her riding-habit.

It was hanging in the wardrobe. So were the few other things she had brought with her.

She put them in the shawl which had been attached to her saddle.

Then she wrapped her slippers and her hair-brush in her blue chiffon scarf.

When she was ready, she peeped through the curtains.

To her relief she saw there was a moon that was turning everything outside to silver.

It would make it easier for her to find her way to the stables.

She would collect Mercury and ride away.

Very, very softly, she opened the door of her bedroom.

On tip-toe she went down the stairs.

Everything was silent.

She thought that if one of the wooden stairs creaked it would be like a pistol-shot.

There was moonlight coming from two glass windows on either side of the door.

As she reached it she saw there were two bolts one up high, the other low down.

She had to balance on tip-toe to reach the higher bolt.

She was just drawing it back finding it rather stiff when a voice behind her asked:

"Where do you think you are going?"

She started and turned round.

In the moonlight she could see Nikōs standing at the top of the stairs.

He was wearing the crimson robe he had worn when he came to her room.

He came down the stairs towards her.

She felt he was very large and overpowering, while she was like a School-girl, who had been caught out playing truant.

He came nearer.

Just as he reached the last step she turned round to stand at the window with her back to him.

She thought he was going to be angry and she was trembling.

"I have . . to go! I . . have to go . . away!" she told herself.

Then Nikōs was just behind her and to her surprise his voice was quiet and gentle as he asked:

"Why are you leaving me?"

"I . . I have . . to!"

"Why?"

she tried to find words and because she did not speak Nikōs asked again:

"Why are you going?"

Thea told the truth.

"Because . . I want to . . stay with . . you."

For a moment there was silence, before he said:

"My darling, I was a fool to frighten you."

He drew in his breath, then almost as if he was speaking to himself he said:

"I had no idea that you were so young, so innocent, so unspoilt!"

"I . . I have to . . go," Thea said. "I will . . find somewhere . . else to . . stay."

"You really think I would let you do anything so dangerous?" Nikōs asked. "So incredibly foolish?"

Because his voice was so kind and because she was still frightened, once again Thea was crying.

Nikōs did not say any more, he merely bent and picked her up in his arms.

Clutching her two bundles against her breast, Thea put her head against his shoulder and shut her eyes.

She was aware of the security of his arms, the comfort of being close to him.

The world outside was dark and she was sure there were Dragons waiting to hurt her.

Nikōs carried her up the stairs, and back into her bedroom.

He set her gently down on the bed and taking her bundles from her he put them down on a chair.

Then he said:

"I want you to go to sleep. Tomorrow we will make plans, but now you are tired."

"I . . I thought . . you would be . . asleep," Thea stammered.

"I was sitting thinking about you."

"As I . . thought about . . you."

"I think, my darling," he said, "you were loving me, as I was loving you."

Thea looked at him with wide eyes.

"How . . how do you . . know . . that?"

He smiled.

"We know so much about each other, how could you possibly do anything so cruel, so wrong and wicked as to leave me?"

She knew he was quoting her own words at her.

She wanted to stay because it had been an agony to have to run away.

Instinctively she put out her hands towards him, and he took them in his.

"I am going to say now," he said very quietly, "something I swear to you I have never said to any other woman."

He looked at her for a long moment.

"I love you! I love you, Thea, as I never thought it would be possible for me to love anybody!"

Thea drew in her breath.

In a very small voice he could hardly hear she whispered:

"I . . I have . . only just . . realised that . . what I . . am feeling . . is love!"

Chapter Four

Thea was called in the morning by Valou's wife.

She was a large, fat woman with what must once have been a very pretty face and an engaging smile.

She pulled back the curtains, put a cup of chocolate down beside the bed and said:

"It's a lovely morning, *Fräulein*, and it'll be hot later."

She brought in a can of hot water and put it on the wash-hand stand.

Later Thea went downstairs a little shyly. She had put on the skirt of her habit, but not the jacket.

As she expected, the breakfast was laid on the balcony and Nikōs was already there.

He looked, she thought, as he rose to his feet exceedingly handsome.

She sat down beside him with a little murmur.

Géza immediately brought her hot coffee.

To her surprise, there was also a dish of eggs. It was what her father always had at the Palace.

Nikōs must have known from her expression that it was not what she expected, for he said:

"I ordered something substantial to eat because we are going riding."

Thea's eyes lit up.

"That is what I want!"

"And so do I," he replied. "So hurry, because Mercury and Isten are waiting for us."

"Is that the name of your horse?"

"Yes, he is called after a god who was worshipped by the Hungarians in the seventh century."

"I look forward to meeting him," Thea smiled.

"I am waiting to see how you ride," Nikōs replied.

She knew he was teasing her, but at the same time she avoided meeting his eyes.

She thought she had behaved last night in a very uncontrolled and foolish fashion. She was sure he was condemning her for not having more pride.

Then, as she finished her eggs, he said very quietly:

"I have not forgotten to tell you that you look very lovely this morning."

She looked away from him as he went on:

"You are like the water-lily buds we saw yesterday in the forest and I long, as I have never longed for anything, to see you in bloom!"

She thought he meant when he made love to her and she blushed.

Nikōs rose to his feet.

"Get your jacket," he advised, "although I doubt if you will need it. The horses are waiting for us."

Thea ran upstairs, but when she went to take down her jacket from the wardrobe where it was hanging, she had a better idea.

She thought the jacket would get creased if it was attached to Mercury's saddle.

Also it would be too constraining to wear if they were riding far.

Instead she opened a drawer to find the shawl in which she had wrapped her clothes when she had left the Palace.

It was of a very fine wool.

It had been beautifully knitted by one of the women in Gyula, who were noted for their skill.

With a long fringe it was very graceful.

When she wore it she felt she was like the dancers who sometimes performed in the City.

She put the shawl over her arm and went downstairs.

Outside at the back of the house the horses were waiting.

The moment Thea appeared, Mercury gave a whinny of delight and nuzzled against her as he always did.

She patted him saying in a low, coaxing voice:

"How are you, my dearest? Are you rested? And did they give you plenty to eat?"

Valou laughed.

"He ate enough, Gracious Lady, for half-a-dozen horses!"

"Thank you for taking care of him," Thea said.

Then she looked at Nikōs's horse and gave a gasp of astonishment.

If Mercury was spectacular, so was Isten.

He was a white stallion, over 16 hands high, and bigger than Mercury.

There was no doubt there was Arab blood in him.

There was not a single patch of colour on the whole of his body.

Nikōs laughed at her surprise, and he said:

"Let me introduce you to Isten, who is enjoying your admiration."

"How can I find words to tell him how magnificent he is?" Thea asked.

"I am sure he can read your thoughts – as I do," Nikōs replied.

As he spoke he lifted her into the saddle.

She felt a little thrill like sunshine run through her at the touch of his hands. For a moment his face was very near to hers.

Having settled her in the saddle, he then arranged her skirt over the stirrup.

76

When it was done to his satisfaction he looked up at her.

Their eyes met and Thea was conscious of her love moving in her breast towards him.

Almost abruptly, Nikōs turned away and mounted Isten.

They moved off, riding from the house and into the woods.

Because the path was a narrow one, Nikōs led the way.

After they had ridden for a little while between the trees, they began to descend.

It was down a twisting track into the valley.

He did not hurry, and when they reached the level ground below, Thea saw it was a perfect place for riding.

It was like the Steppes she had galloped over yesterday.

Now she could ride side by side with Nikōs and as she glanced at him she realised it was what he wanted.

They urged their mounts forward.

Then they were galloping at an incredibly fast pace, speeding over the grassland.

Flights of butterflies rose at their approach. A cloud of small birds flew out of their way.

The stallions, straining to keep up with each other, carried them faster and faster.

They galloped for nearly two miles before the horses, as satisfied as they were, slowed their pace.

Thea turned towards Nikōs.

Her cheeks were flushed, her eyes were shining as if the sun was captured in them.

"That was wonderful!" she cried. "Faster than I have ever ridden in my whole life!"

"You ride exactly as I expected you would," Nikōs said.

"Like a Hungarian?" she laughed.

"Of course!" he agreed. "I only hope you will emulate some of their other characteristics!"

"Which one in particular?" Thea asked lightly.

He did not reply, but when she looked at him she knew the answer.

How often, she wondered, had she heard people say:

"The Hungarians are the most passionate lovers in the world!"

She could not mistake the expression in Nikōs's eyes and quickly she looked away.

As they rode on she was vividly conscious of how handsome he was.

He sat a horse better than any man she had ever seen.

She had thought Georgi was exceptional.

But Nikōs had an authority, at the same time an indefinable way of riding which made him part of his horse.

They rode on.

Thea was utterly content to be riding with the man she loved as she had in her dreams.

There was no need to say anything.

She only knew that everything seemed more beautiful, more alive than it had ever been before.

The flowers seemed more colourful, the sky more blue, the haze on the horizon more magical, just because she was in love.

"How can I have been so foolish as to try to leave him?" she asked herself.

As if she had spoken aloud Nikōs said:

"It is something I will never allow you to do! I cannot lose you, Thea!"

There was a depth to his voice that made her quiver.

Because she was afraid of their being serious, she said laughingly:

"If you read my thoughts, there will be no reason for me to talk."

"Why should we," he asked, "when we can feel?"

She did not reply and he went on:

"I can feel you so vividly beside me, that I know now what I have always missed in the past."

Thea drew in her breath.

"It was you!" he went on. "And now we have found each other, you fill the whole world."

It was what she was thinking herself and she knew that love had changed the world as she knew it.

Now everything was dazzlingly irresistible, pulsating with life.

At the same time, so mysterious and magical that it was exactly what she expected from her Fairy-Stories.

They rode on.

As the sun rose higher and grew hotter, Thea began to feel thirsty.

"Where are we going?" she asked.

She realised as she spoke that it was strange that she had not asked the question before, but it had not seemed to matter.

"I am taking you to enjoy a very different luncheon from what you had yesterday," Nikōs replied.

She looked at him questioningly, and he said:

"It is a surprise, but I think it is one you will appreciate!"

About half-an-hour later they turned into a thick wood.

Now there were no fir-trees, but huge oaks, maples and ash.

Their branches were covered with Spring leaves, a welcome protection from the rays of the sun.

The track between the trees was narrow, and once again Nikōs went ahead.

There was no sound save the song of the birds and the jingle of harness.

Thea thought they must have reached the centre of the wood when they came to a clearing.

As she looked ahead she gave a little exclamation of excitement.

In a circle, under the protection of the trees, there were a number of Gypsy caravans.

Painted in brilliant colours, they looked almost like flowers, so did the women who ran eagerly to greet Nikōs.

They spoke to him in Romany and he answered them in their own language.

Thea was glad she could understand.

"We privileged, Honourable Sir, very honoured you come to visit us again," they were saying, "but how you know we here?"

"A little bird told me," Nikōs replied, and they laughed.

He introduced Thea.

"This is a beautiful lady who is staying with me," he said, "and she loves music!"

Thea felt her heart leap with excitement.

She knew without being told that these were Hungarian Gypsies.

Although the Gypsies came to Kostas, they more often came from the South where they were not pure Hungarians.

Nikōs dismounted.

A Gypsy boy took his stallion to where there was some grass for grazing and he lifted Thea from her saddle.

Once again she thrilled as he did so. She thought he held her a little longer than was necessary before he set her on her feet.

She had already knotted the reins on Mercury's neck, and without being led he followed Isten to where he could graze.

"Now," Nikōs said, "we are hungry!"

He was looking as he spoke at a pot.

It was suspended over a fire in the centre of the clearing.

Thea was already aware of the fragrant aroma coming from it.

The Gypsies brought out chairs for them.

One was the ceremonial chair in which the Voivode Gypsy Chief sat.

The other was sometimes offered to an important guest.

They were made mostly of stags' horns carved and decorated with pieces of gold and silver.

As she sat down Thea thought her chair was worthy of a Queen.

Then she thrust the thought from her.

If she sat on a throne, it would be King Otho's.

She knew that, now she was in love, she would rather die than marry an old man.

If he tried to kiss her, as Nikōs had done, it would be a degradation she could not contemplate.

Nikōs's hand was on hers.

"I will not let you look unhappy," he said in a low voice. "The Gypsy music is full of love, and that is what I want you to feel."

She felt the sunshine invading her, because he was touching her hand.

When she looked into his eyes she knew he wanted to kiss her.

With an effort she forced herself to attend to the Gypsy women.

They looked very attractive in their colourful gowns while coins that hung from the veils over their hair sparkled in the sunlight.

They brought Thea and Nikōs plates piled high with the stew they had cooked over the fire.

As soon as Thea tasted it she realised how delicious it was.

She was sure it was a mixture of roe deer, hare and partridge.

They had cooked it with herbs that grew naturally on the plain and in the woods.

While they were eating, the Gypsies sat down on the ground at their feet.

They were joined by the men who with their high cheekbones, black eyes and jet black hair, looked as if they had come from the East.

That was true, Thea remembered.

The Gypsies had originally come from India and had travelled West to Egypt, on to Hungary and North to Russia.

When everyone had been served with the stew, the Voivode rose to his feet.

As he lifted his violin to his chin there was silence.

At first he played alone, and there was a passionate, mystical note in his music.

Then gradually the other gypsies joined him.

A cymbal, a flageolet, bass, viol, 'cello and half-a-dozen violins blended harmoniously together.

To Thea it was sheer magic, as were the Gypsies themselves.

They had small, regular, delicate features, and sensitive mouths in their dark faces.

Their hands were long and slim, their limbs graceful, lithe and muscular.

The music changed from soft romantic tones to become the *Csárdás*.

Thea had heard it before, but never in such perfect surroundings or as well played as now.

It was the traditional Hungarian dance and comprised all a Gypsy's ambitions and fears, the passion which could become an intolerable sadness.

The bows of the Gypsies were flashing over the strings.

The music tumbled and fell before the pace accelerated.

Thea felt as if she could not breathe.

As if Nikōs felt the same, he took her hand in his.

She knew then the music was saying what was in his heart, it was telling her of his passion for her.

His love for her was wild, passionate and compelling and the sounds seemed to throb through her.

As the music rose up into the sky, she felt it engulfed her, and her feelings rose with it.

Her breath was coming quickly from between her parted lips.

She felt her heart beating frantically in her breast, and Nikōs's fingers tightened on hers.

He wanted to crush her against him, he wanted to kiss her so that she surrendered herself completely.

She knew that was what she wanted him to do.

The music came not only from the Gypsies but from herself and was linked with the music from Nikōs. It told her they were one person.

"I love you! You are mine!"

She did not know whether she heard Nikōs say it in his deep voice or whether she listened to it with her heart.

She only knew her whole body as well as her mind was crying out to him.

"I . . love you! I love . . you!"

The music came to a sudden climax.

Then the wild movement slipped into a slow, soft rhythm.

It gave Thea a chance to breathe again, but she knew that she had experienced something overwhelmingly emotional.

It was what Nikōs had wanted her to feel.

The Gypsies were playing again and now several of the girls and young men began to dance.

It was very graceful and very beautiful.

At the same time it was not the music of passion which had excited Thea in a way she had never been excited before.

It made her shy to think of what she had felt.

She was aware that Nikōs was watching her and she

knew he had brought her here because he had wanted her to feel wild as the wind.

It was the sensation he had given her last night when he had kissed her neck and when he had held her completely captive with his lips.

She took her hand from his and clasped her fingers together.

She knew this was what she would feel if he made love to her, as he had wanted to do.

"How . . can I resist . . him?" she asked herself.

Then she was ashamed that she should think anything so wrong and what her mother would say was a sin.

The Gypsies' dance came to an end and the dancers flung themselves down in an abandoned manner at Nikōs's feet.

"You are pleased, gracious Sir?"

"Very pleased!" Nikōs replied.

He brought his purse from his pocket and gave all those who had performed a coin.

Thea thought the coins were gold.

She wondered if he was rich enough to afford it.

The Gypsy girls kissed his hand, the men bowed and thanked him.

"Now we must leave," Nikōs said. "It is a long way home and the heat of the sun is over."

He looked up at the sky as he spoke.

Thea realised they had taken hours eating, listening to the music and watching the dancing.

It must now be getting on for four o'clock.

She called to Mercury and he came to her at once, while Isten was led by a Gypsy-boy to his Master.

Nikōs lifted Thea into the saddle.

She was still stirred by the music and she wanted to put her head on his shoulder and shut her eyes.

She wished he would take her home on the front of his saddle.

Instead she just said 'thank you' in her soft voice.

She felt he would know that she was thanking him for everything that had happened.

The Gypsies started to cry out their farewells.

As they did so the Voivode who had played the violin first picked it up again.

He started a gay, romantic tune which seemed to have been composed especially to speed lovers on their journey.

Long after they were out of sight of the camp Thea could still hear the music in the distance.

She felt it was carried to them by the movements of the leaves overhead.

Soon they were on flat ground.

Then they were galloping as they had on the way out, but not so wildly nor so swiftly.

Thea was sure Nikōs was slowing his own pace so that she would not feel tired.

They left the plain as they had before and rode up the twisting road which led them to the fir-trees.

As they reached the top Nikōs moved ahead.

Thea was suddenly aware of a number of men who came from behind the trees and encircled them.

Because her eyes were still dazzled by the light in the plain, she could hardly see them.

They were little more than dark shadows.

Then she heard Nikōs speaking in a voice which she knew was one of hostility: with a stab of fear she realised that the men were Bandits.

Everybody in Kostas knew of the gang of Bandits which moved about the Balkan mountains. They were a menace to every country they visited.

They stole sheep and goats, horses were spirited away.

Often, it was whispered, young women vanished too.

Every Ruler, including her father, had tried to capture them.

But it always took time before the people in the City were aware of what they were doing to the farmers and stock-breeders near the mountains.

By the time the soldiers came to search for them, they had always vanished.

Thea had heard so often what they looked like.

Their sheep-skin capes, their strange, hard faces and the weapons they carried in their waist-bands.

She saw how their long, dark, untidy hair was not covered with the exception of the man who, she thought, must be their leader.

He was speaking to Nikōs who was arguing with him.

They were speaking a different language to the one Nikōs had used to Valou.

Thea did not at first understand them.

Then she realised that the Bandit spoke a mixture of Albanian, Greek and Turkish and she began to get the sense of what was being said.

The Chief was demanding a ransom.

She knew then with horror that the Bandits intended to take them prisoner.

She edged her horse nearer to Nikōs. As she did so she was aware how angry he was.

The Bandit Chief gave an order. Two men moved forward to hold onto the bridles of Isten and Mercury.

Immediately the horses reared.

"Do not touch our animals!" Nikōs said sharply. "We will follow you – as we have no other choice."

"They not your animals for long!" the Bandit Chief replied derisively. "They good horses!"

Nikōs did not reply but Thea gave a cry of horror.

How could she let Mercury be taken from her by men like these?

She looked desperately at Nikōs and she could see how furious he was.

But he said to her quietly:

"We have to go with them, but it will be all right."

"How can it be?" Thea answered in horror.

Then she realised he was speaking in English so that the Bandits would not understand.

She had never imagined that he would be able to speak English, as she could.

She answered in a frightened little voice:

"What . . can we . . do? How can . . I lose . . Mercury?"

"Trust me," Nikōs said. "I should have anticipated that something like this would happen."

She knew he felt helpless because he had no pistol with him.

She was aware, without his telling her so, that there was nothing he could do against a dozen Bandits. And all the less since she was with him.

If he had been alone, he might have somehow managed to gallop away.

He could have taken the risk that they would not shoot at a horse as magnificent as Isten.

But it was a risk he dare not take with her.

The Bandit Chief was leading the way through the trees.

With a sinking of her heart Thea knew it was in the opposite direction to Nikōs's house.

Now they were moving upwards and they had to go slowly.

It was a rocky surface and the horses might slip.

After what seemed a long time they came to what was a plateau of rock.

The mountains towered above them but there were caves on each side of the plateau.

Thea realised it was a perfect hiding-place for the Bandits.

As they appeared other men, women and small children came from the caves.

The men were dressed in the same way with guns and daggers at their waists.

Some of the women wore the vivid skirts of the peasants.

They all wore brightly coloured head-scarfs and each woman was ornamented with a great deal of jewellery.

Their huge earrings, bracelets and a variety of necklaces seemed strange against their dirty ragged garments.

They clustered around Thea, staring up at her.

She thought how different they were from the beauty and grace of the Gypsies.

The Bandit Chief said something to Nikōs, and he dismounted slowly.

Then he lifted Thea down from the saddle and as he did so, she clung to him, saying in English:

"Y.you will not . . leave me?"

"Of course not," he replied.

She felt that while he was reassuring her, he was, at the same time, anxious.

The men would have led Mercury away.

Nikōs stopped them sharply with a word of command and he took Thea's shawl from where it had been tied to the saddle and wrapped it round her shoulders.

She was glad of the warmth as they were very high up.

It was much cooler and she knew it would be very cold later when darkness came.

"How . . can we . . stay here? What . . will they . . do to . . us?" she asked herself frantically.

Because she was afraid she slipped her hand into Nikōs's.

She felt his fingers, warm and strong, giving her a sense of protection.

Now they were standing in the centre of the plateau.

The Bandits were all clustered round them, staring as if they were wild animals rather than human beings.

Then the Bandit Chief began to speak.

"You rich man," he said to Nikōs. "We want 10,000 ducats for you, 5,000 for your woman!"

He paused before he went on:

"You try escape, or soldiers come, we kill! Each day we not receive money, we cut one finger, or one toe!"

Thea would have given a cry of horror but the presence of Nikōs's fingers prevented her from doing so.

She knew he wanted her to be dignified and not let the Bandits know she was afraid.

She thought too, it was how her father would expect her to appear.

She could remember her mother saying:

"Royalty never show their emotions in public, like ordinary people."

"I must . . be Royal! I must be . . Royal!" she said to herself.

Yet she was trembling.

"What I will do," Nikōs was saying, "is to send a note to a friend who will give your messenger the money."

The Bandit was listening.

"I will write the note in your language," Nikōs went on, "so that you can see there are no tricks about it."

"If there tricks – you die!" the Bandit Chief said fiercely.

Nikōs ignored him and searched in his pockets as if for something to write on.

The Bandit Chief gave an order and a man ran to bring him a piece of paper that was more like parchment.

It was none too clean and somewhat creased.

Thea suspected this was not the first time the Bandits had demanded a ransom.

When another man provided an ink-well and a quill pen she was sure of it.

There was a large rock at the side of the plateau and Nikōs stood at it to write.

The ink was thin and the quill-pen badly sharpened.

However he wrote slowly and distinctly.

Standing by him, Thea saw he had put what was wanted into three lines.

Then he signed his name.

She thought as he wrote that at last she would learn his other name but he just signed the paper '*Nikōs*'.

Then he waited for it to dry.

He then turned the paper over on the other side and wrote the address to which it was to be taken.

Not knowing the country, Thea had no idea whether it was far away or near.

She thought with horror that they might be imprisoned for days.

Then she remembered the threat the Bandit Chief had made and it made her want to cry out in sheer terror.

She managed however to stand at Nikōs's side with her chin up.

Before he handed the Bandit the piece of paper, he read it aloud so that everybody could hear him.

He then read out the address and a young Bandit came forward to take the paper.

"I hope you will hurry," Nikōs said.

"He hurry as I want money!" the Bandit Chief said before the messenger could reply.

"And now," Nikōs said, "as it will soon be getting cold, I would be grateful if we, as your prisoners, could be treated generously and be given a cave in which we can be alone."

"*You* have cave," the Bandit Chief replied, "woman stay with us!"

Thea felt as if her heart had stopped beating.

While Nikōs was writing the note she had been aware that some of the younger Bandits had been pointing at her, laughing and whispering amongst themselves.

She thought they were just being rude or perhaps they were comparing to their own women.

But now she was afraid, desperately afraid!

Her hand went out to Nikōs and she knew as she touched him that he was as apprehensive as she was.

She was so panic-stricken that she contemplated running away.

She would run into the wood, hoping she would be able to hide.

Then she knew it was a hopeless idea.

The Bandits would catch her easily.

They would be touching her and her whole body screamed out at the horror of it.

"Oh . . God . . help . . me!" she prayed.

Even as she did so, Nikōs had had an idea.

Perceptively she could see it come into his mind.

She was aware that he drew in his breath and he was calling on some Power stronger than himself.

He seemed suddenly to grow in stature.

He was taller, more authoritative, almost omnipotent.

She could not understand it.

Yet, because they were so closely attuned to each other, she knew it had happened and Nikōs would save her.

He looked around at the Bandits. Then he said to their Chief:

"I have a story to tell you, and I want you all to listen before it grows dark. Call all your people and tell them to sit down on the ground."

Thea thought the Bandit Chief was about to refuse.

She could feel Nikōs concentrating on him.

He was willing him to be obedient to his will.

The two men looked at each other, the Bandit defiantly.

Without speaking but with a force that Thea could feel emanating out of him, Nikōs won the silent battle.

The Bandit's eyes fell before his and he turned round and shouted at his followers.

They were gesticulating, pointing, talking amongst themselves.

Obediently they came towards their leader and sat down as he commanded.

Nikōs did not move.

He just stood with his arm round Thea's shoulders.

The men, women and children squatted until only their Chief was standing.

Thea thought this could not truly be happening.

The rays of the dying sun were touching the peaks of the mountains, and turning the snow to gold.

Even the rocks had a strange glow which was in itself very beautiful.

There was something unreal about the whole scene.

The caves, the rocks, the frightening Bandits and themselves.

The situation was one of sheer terror.

Thea looked up at the sky and saw the first evening star.

It was very faint, but it was there.

Thea knew, incredible though it might seem, they were protected.

It was by the power which Nikōs had just drawn into himself.

Nikōs was waiting.

As if he still had control over the Chief Bandit, the man slowly, reluctantly, sat down.

Then there was silence.

Chapter Five

Thea could feel the tension in the air.

The Chief of the Bandits glared at Nikōs with what she thought was hatred and envy.

Certainly Nikōs looked very different from them.

She was also aware that the younger Bandits were watching her.

She found it difficult to force herself to ignore them.

She managed however, to hold herself proudly.

Only Nikōs's arm around her gave a little comfort and she was praying fervently in her heart:

"Please . . God . . save me . . please . . please . . . !"

She felt her prayer was winging its way up into Heaven.

Then Nikōs began to speak.

"I want to tell you a story," he said in his deep, educated voice.

He was speaking the Bandit's language, but Thea could understand.

"I married my wife, who is here with me, when she was fifteen. Because we were very much in love, we hoped we would have a child."

He glanced for a moment at the Bandits' children.

They might not be very prepossessing, but they were fat and well fed.

"Like all of you," Nikōs continued, "I wanted a son, but alas! We were not lucky."

He sighed and then went on:

"As the years passed I began to be afraid that my name would die with me."

Thea realised that the Bandits were listening intently.

She thought some of them looked rather more sympathetic than they had when Nikōs started.

"A few years ago in desperation," he was saying, "I prayed to Héja, who as you all know, lives on the highest mountain of this land, and reigns over us all."

Thea had heard of Héja.

He was the King of all the gods in the mountains.

She realised by their faces that the Bandits knew of him and doubtless worshipped him.

"I went to the great Cascade," Nikōs went on, "which falls directly from Héja down into the plains, to bring life and fertility to our crops."

One or two of the Bandits murmured as if they were obviously familiar with the Cascade.

Thea thought vaguely that she had heard about it.

She was however not certain into which Kingdom it poured from the mountain tops.

Nearly all of the Balkan countries had similar cascades.

She had the idea that the Cascade of Héja was thought more important than the others.

"Then I had a dream," Nikōs said, "and I knew that Héja was speaking to me."

His voice rose as he said:

"Héja said if when the moon was full, my wife Thea bathed naked in the Cascade, she would conceive a child."

A sound of surprise came from the Bandits, and Thea herself was astonished.

"My wife is now with child," Nikōs declared dramatically "In five months I believe I shall have the son I need so urgently."

There was silence for a moment.

Then in a voice that sounded almost, Thea thought, like the roar of thunder he declaimed:

"It is Héja's child she carries! Héja, King of the Gods! If anyone should touch her, insult or defile her, they will be cursed!"

There was a dramatic silence from the Bandits and several of the women crossed themselves.

"You all know," Nikōs said, "the vengeance of the gods, but you also know they can bless and protect you."

His arm tightened round Thea as he said:

"You have been blessed because my wife Thea is here amongst you. Let her stay unmolested and in peace, otherwise Héja will take his revenge!"

Nikōs's voice rang out.

When he finished speaking the sun had vanished below the horizon. The light faded from the snow on the mountain tops.

To Thea it seemed that they were in darkness.

Then as if he must break the tension, the Chief Bandit rose.

He gave an order and the Bandits thrust thick tar-tipped sticks into the fire.

Then there was light.

Nikōs and Thea did not move.

The Bandit Chief said in a surly tone:

"I show you cave where you wait 'til my messenger returns."

"Thank you," Nikōs said quietly.

He and Thea followed him across the plateau.

They had taken only a few steps when the women rushed forward carrying or dragging their small children with them.

They knelt before Thea.

"Bless us," they begged, "give us the blessing of Héja."

For a moment Thea could only stare at them wide eyed.

Then Nikōs said quietly in English:

"Put your hand on their heads, and say a prayer."

She was too frightened to do anything but obey him.

She touched the children.

As she did so she said a simple prayer, which was one her Mother had always used when she prayed at her knee.

"May God and the Angels bless you and watch over you now and for your whole life."

She soon had blessed all the children, there being not very many of them.

Then the women beseeched her.

"I lost my last two babies," one said. "Bless me, that the next will be born strong."

Thea felt that what she was doing was almost sacrilegious.

She looked at Nikōs.

"Pray that she will have a son. That is all she asks for," he said quitely.

Thea put her hands over the head of the woman.

"May God bless you, and give you the son you long for, may he be strong, brave and at the same time kind and merciful."

The woman bent and kissed Thea's feet.

Then Thea blessed the other women until Nikōs drew away to where the Chief Bandit was waiting.

She saw as they moved that the young men who had looked at her with lecherous eyes had disappeared.

Nikōs had won.

The cave was dark, and rather frightening.

One of the flares however was fixed outside, so that they could just see.

There was a pile of dried leaves against one wall, the floor was sandy, and Thea thought there was a faint smell of chamois, or perhaps a wolf.

But nothing mattered except that she would be with Nikōs and thanks to his presence of mind the Bandits would not dare to touch her.

Then as if they must show their gratitude, or perhaps their reverence, the Bandit women came hurrying in.

They brought a blanket to lay over the dried leaves.

It was none too clean, but at least, Thea thought, it would prevent their being pricked.

She was certain there would be brambles and thorns amongst the leaves.

There were two other blankets with which to cover themselves. Also a rough pillow which looked more lumpy than soft.

The blankets were torn, but Thea was aware that it was the best they could do.

She thanked them a little hesitatingly in their own language.

Nikōs thanked them too.

Then because it was now dark outside, the Bandits withdrew and Thea knew they were going to their caves to sleep.

The Bandit Chief however said before he went:

"You try escape – we shoot you!"

It was as if he wanted to assert himself, feeling that Nikōs's ascendancy over his followers had humiliated him.

"We will be here when it is light," Nikōs replied.

With a sound that was like a grunt the Bandit walked away.

It was then Thea flung herself against Nikōs saying:

"You saved me . . you were wonderful! How could . . you be so . . clever?"

He put his arms around her and replied quietly:

"We are safe for the moment, but I want you now to lie down and rest."

She looked at the bed and was aware as she did so that it was growing very cold outside.

Now that the sun had gone down the temperature had dropped dramatically.

She knew, because they were so high up, that the snow was only just above them.

With what she thought was a note of amusement in his voice Nikōs said:

"I think, my darling, we would be very unwise if we did not rest close together."

"You . . will not . . leave me?" Thea said almost as if he had suggested it.

"That is something I shall not be allowed to do," Nikōs replied. "Instead, if I hold you in my arms, you will be warm, and you will feel very much safer."

Because she knew he was being sensible, Thea moved towards the bed.

It was more comfortable than she expected.

As she lay against the side of the cave so that Nikōs would be on the outside, she found she was quite warm.

The blankets were made of a thick wool from the mountain sheep.

She seemed to sink into the leaves beneath her.

She was wearing her woollen shawl.

Only when Nikōs joined her did she remember for the first time that he was not wearing a coat.

He had expected to be back in the cosy warmth of his little house by this time.

They would be sitting in front of the log fire as they had done last night.

He lay down and put his arm around her and she said:

"I am afraid . . you will be very . . cold."

"I am relying on you to keep me warm," he replied.

He had spread the blankets over them up to their waists, and now he pulled them even higher.

As he did so Thea spread the end of her shawl across his chest, thinking even a little of its warmth was better than nothing.

Then Nikōs put his ohter arm around her.

As she rested her head on his shoulder she thought how she had wanted to be close to him like this.

It seemed extraordinary that it was the Bandits who had made it possible.

"All that matters is that we are together," she thought.

"Yes, we are together," Nikōs said as if he read her thoughts, "and you are not to be afraid, my darling."

"I thought when you were speaking so cleverly that the Bandits believed you," Thea said, "but if we had to die, at least I was with you!"

"We are not going to die," he said in his deep voice. "We are going to live, my precious, and we shall look back on this as an adventure which we will tell our children and our grandchildren."

Because she was shy, Thea gave a little murmur and turned her face against him.

She felt him kiss her hair, then he said very quietly:

"Will you marry me, my darling? I know now that I cannot live without you."

For a moment Thea was still.

That Nikōs should want to marry her was the most incredible and yet the most marvellous thing that could ever happen.

She knew too that it was impossible and it was something she would never be allowed to do.

Then she asked herself – why not?

If she was married to Nikōs it would then be impossible for her to become King Otho's wife.

She was also aware that she could no longer be Royal.

She knew how furious her father would be but if she was legally married there would be nothing he could do about it.

She remembered what had happened to a distant cousin.

She had been Royal, the youngest daughter of the King of Tek.

Her sisters, and there were three of them, were all married to reigning Monarchs, but she had fallen in love with one of her father's *Aides-de-camp*.

They had run away together.

Her father the King had stripped her of her Royal rank and her name had been erased from the Royal heirarchy.

Thea had been told that she was never spoken of again.

She had often wondered if giving up everything, losing her Royal rank and status, had been worth it.

Now she knew that if it was a choice between being a Princess and a Queen as the wife of King Otho or renouncing it all for Nikōs, there was no question as to what she would answer.

She loved Nikōs as he loved her.

They were closely attuned like the notes of two violins. They were incomplete without each other.

The thought flashed through her mind that if she was married to Nikōs, she need never go back to the Palace.

If the soldiers did not find her, then in time she would be presumed dead.

If they did find her and she was married to Nikōs, there would be nothing they could do about it.

Except that she would no longer be Princess Sydel.

Nikōs was waiting, but he did not move.

His lips did not touch hers, but she could hear his heart beating.

She raised her head to look up at him.

She could see him in the light that came from the flare outside which was burning lower.

"I love . . you!" she said.

"Then you will marry me?"

"I can . . imagine nothing more . . wonderful than to be . . your wife!"

It was then she knew he had been tense as he waited for her answer.

Now their bodies seemed to melt into each others, and he held her so close that she could hardly breathe.

Then he said:

"That is what I wanted you to say, and I swear to you, my lovely little goddess, I will make you happy."

"I love you!" Thea said again. "All I can think of is you . . and your . . love."

"That is all I want you to think about," Nikōs said, "and we will be married immediately we are free."

Thea gave a little shudder.

"You do . . not think that they will . . hurt us?"

"Not if they receive the money they have asked for."

"There will be . . no difficulty about . . that?"

She was terribly afraid he might say he had not got so much money, but he replied:

"Do not think about it, think only that in a very short while I shall be able to make love to you, as I want to do."

Thea thought of last night and blushed, and she was glad he could not see her face.

She wanted him to kiss her.

She wanted him to give her the ecstasy and the rapture that she had felt before. Foolishly she had been frightened and had sent him away.

"When we are married," Nikōs said, as if he was following his own train of thought, "I will teach you, my precious little Ice Maiden, about love, but now you must be kind to me."

"Kind?" Thea asked.

"You know that I dare not kiss you."

"But . . why not?" Thea asked.

She lifted her lips and knew that they were very near to his.

She wanted his kisses; she wanted them desperately.

Nikōs's arms tightened.

"Last night," he said, "I frightened you, and I knew afterwards that it was very foolish of me."

He drew in his breath before he said:

"You have no idea how beautiful you looked when I came to your bedroom, with your amazing hair falling over your shoulders, your eyes green as emeralds in the light from the candles."

The way he spoke made Thea quiver.

As Nikōs was aware of it, he went on:

"Because we both have Hungarian blood in us, we come from the sun. We are easily aroused and our passions burn fiercely and demandingly, like the heat of the sun itself!"

The way he was speaking was very exciting and Thea moved a little closer to him.

"I want you, my lovely one, I want you unbearably, uncontrollably. I want to kiss you from the top of your head to the toes of your tiny feet."

There was a note of wild passion in his voice.

It reminded Thea of the music of the Gypsies and she felt a flame awake within herself and move from her breast towards her lips.

"But because I will also revere and worship you as my wife," Nikōs continued, "I will not make you mine until we receive the blessing of the Church and are joined by God in a bond which no man can sever."

The way he spoke was very moving.

She felt her love seeping through her and her heart beating frantically against his.

"Would it . . matter very much if you just . . kissed me?" she asked.

"You must not tempt me!"

"Tempt . . you?"

"You do not understand," he said. "I adore your innocence and your ignorance about love, but I am also a man, Thea!"

'A magnificent, an heroic man,' she thought.

Who else would have shown such courage as he had shown when the Bandits surrounded them?

Who else could have held them spellbound? Who else could have saved her from the degradation and horror of what they intended?

"You are . . wonderful!" she said. "So wonderful that I am . . afraid you will . . find me dull as . . your wife."

She thought of the monotonous, uneventful days and years she had spent at the Palace.

The conversation of the Courtiers was so dreary that she had ceased to listen to them.

With Nikōs everything had been a delight, exciting, stimulating, and enthralling!

Now, close in his arms, even the Bandits outside with their threats did not seem so frightening.

Nikōs was holding her safe against him and in some strange way he seemed to have a dominance over them.

"What I want you to do," he was saying, and now his voice was no longer vibrant with passion, "is to go to sleep. Tomorrow, when the ransom has been paid, we will return home to our little house and arrange our marriage."

She knew he was watching over her and because she loved him she must do as he asked.

"I will just say . . my prayers," she said, "and . . thank God that I am . . with . . you."

She thought of how terrifying it would have been if she had been riding alone, then she had encountered the Bandits!

They would certainly have taken her prisoner, if only because they wished to steal Mercury.

The younger Bandits would have been waiting for her.

If Nikōs had not been there to save her, what might have happened?

She shivered.

103

"Forget it!" Nikōs said. "Forget everything except that the stars are watching over us."

"And Héja?" Thea enquired.

"He is the King of all the gods who dwell in the mountains," Nikōs replied, "and who knows that better than you?"

He was teasing her and she gave a little laugh.

"After the way you spoke about him I believe in him implicitly, as the Bandits do. How can they live up here and not be aware of the god above them?"

"They are in fact a very superstitious people," Nikōs explained.

"I know that . . now," Thea said, "and that we . . were very . . lucky!"

"Very lucky indeed!" Nikōs said quietly. "And now, my darling, go to sleep."

"I am trying to do as you tell me," Thea said, "but it is very exciting being so close to you."

"How do you think I feel?" Nikōs enquired.

The passion was back in his voice.

As if with a superhuman effort he controlled himself and said:

"Go to sleep."

Thea said her prayers.

Then because she was very tired with all the emotions of last night and the happenings of the day, she gradually relaxed.

Nikōs could hear her breathing evenly.

The torch outside had finally burnt away.

Now there was only the light from the moon and the stars.

He looked through the opening in the cave at the rocks which the moon had turned to silver.

From the way he was lying he could just see some stars like diamonds in the sky.

He told himself that, whatever the difficulties ahead, he would protect and take care of Thea.

She was so beautiful.

It was incredible that he had found the one woman in the whole world who was the completion of himself.

He was wise enough to know that it was almost an impossibility.

Yet he knew what Thea was thinking, and she too seemed to know his thoughts.

There was an affinity between them which was miraculous.

All through his life he had believed in a Power which had helped him when he needed it most.

He had called on it tonight when he had known better than Thea did what the Bandits intended.

Women to them were of complete unimportance except for amusement and the breeding of sons.

Thea had heard of the Bandits stealing away peasant girls.

That was only part of the story.

Nikōs knew that many of the girls they carried away with them into the mountains were brutally ill-treated.

They became half-mad with the terror of what they had endured.

Then they would either throw themselves voluntarily down the mountainside or else were thrown into a chasm by the Bandits themselves.

Only a few of their own women survived to cook for them and to tend them if they were wounded.

But they were of less importance than the mountain ponies which carried their ill-gotten gains.

That he had managed to save Thea was, he believed, a miracle.

It came from the God in Whom he believed, and Who had never failed him.

What mattered in the future was that he had found Thea.

He loved her with an intensity he had never thought possible.

She had come into his life as swiftly as the starlight appeared in the sky.

He vowed he would never lose her or let her leave him.

"She is mine!" he said.

He spoke fiercely as if he was fighting a battle for her.

Thea was asleep when she heard the sound of voices.

As she stirred and came back to consciousness, there was the sound of gunfire.

She opened her eyes.

As she did so Nikōs took his arms from her and got to his feet.

"What . . is . . happening?" Thea asked and she was frightened.

Nikōs straightened himself.

The cave was just high enough for him to be able to stand upright.

The noise outside increased.

Now through the opening of the cave Thea could see that dawn had broken and the sky was light.

Nikōs walked without hurrying to the entrance of the cave and looked out.

More shots were being fired and the sound was almost deafening.

Thea sat up.

"I . . I am afraid . . Oh, Nikōs . . what is . . happening?"

He turned back to her to say:

"Stay where you are! Do not move, and do not look out, do you understand?"

It was an order.

Thea tried to collect her thoughts and to ask again what was happening.

Then she saw him move forward and disappear.

She gave an involuntary cry of horror but it was too late to stop him.

She was desperately afraid that if the Bandits were shooting they might shoot at him.

'Supposing,' she thought, 'if Nikōs is killed and I am left . . alone?'

She wanted to run after him, to be sure that if, as she had thought before, he died, she would die too.

Now there were no more shots.

Without moving she thought she could hear Nikōs's voice.

Then she could hear him clearly.

His voice was calm and authoritative, and she knew he was giving orders.

"What can be happening?" she asked herself.

Because there was nothing else that she could do, she started to pray.

She prayed desperately because she was so frightened.

"Please . . God . . do not let them . . hurt him . . please, God . . keep him safe . . I cannot . . lose him now . . please, God . . please . . . !"

She shut her eyes and she was also afraid to listen.

At last, and it seemed to her a very long time, she heard somebody coming into the cave.

She opened her eyes.

For a moment, because she was frightened, it was impossible to see.

A man was blocking out the light.

Then she saw that it was Nikōs.

She gave a cry of happiness and relief.

He bent down and lifted her off the bed on which they had slept.

When he did so he saw how pale she was and fear had made her eyes dark.

"It is all right, my darling," he said softly. "It is over, and now we can go home."

"H . . how . . what . . what has . . happened?" Thea stammered.

In answer he drew her to the mouth of the cave.

It was a few feet higher than the plateau.

She could see to her astonishment that there were soldiers everywhere, quite a number of them. They looked very smart in their red coats in contrast to the Bandits.

The Bandits now looked even more desreputable and unpleasant than they had the night before.

They were all being marched down the path up which they had brought Thea and Nikōs.

None protested.

Thea was sure they had fired at the soldiers, who had fired back.

There were four Bandits injured. They were lying or sitting on the plateau with blood on their legs, hands and arms.

Thea stood staring at what she saw.

Then with an inexpressible joy, she saw two soldiers leading Mercury and Isten.

"Mercury is . . safe!" she murmured.

"And so are you, my darling!" Nikōs replied.

He helped her down from the cave and onto the plateau.

She went at once to Mercury and as he nuzzled against her she asked:

"You do not think they have hurt him?"

Nikōs asked the same question of the soldiers who shook their heads and replied:

"Only the saddles are damaged, *Mein Herr*."

Thea looked at her saddle.

She saw that the leather had been slashed. She supposed the Bandits had done so in order to look inside it.

"They were searching for money," Nikōs explained, "but I think it will carry you home."

He lifted her up as he spoke and placed her in the saddle.

Then he walked across the plateau.

Thea could see there was an Officer superintending the removal of the Bandits.

Nikōs talked to him for a long time.

Thea could not hear what they were saying and she had no wish to.

She was patting Mercury, happy that he was unhurt.

She knew how agonising it would have been for her if he had been killed when the soldiers arrived.

She wondered how they could have learnt that this was where they were being held captive.

She supposed it must have been the ransom note which had told them.

At the same time, she thought that the Bandits who had carried it could not have got very far.

She expected that Nikōs would explain everything to her later.

As she looked at him thinking how handsome he was and how much she loved him, the sun rose.

The Bandits had disappeared down the path.

Now she saw the officer salute Nikōs, then hurry down the path after his men and their prisoners.

Nikōs came back to her.

He mounted Isten and thanked the soldier who had been holding him.

Then he smiled at Thea and said:

"Now we can go home."

There was a note in his voice that told Thea how much it meant to him.

The little house would be their home, where she would live as his wife.

His eyes were on her lips and she felt as if he kissed her.

Then with a feeling like the music of the birds in her breast she said:

"That . . is wonderful . . absolutely . . wonderful!"

Chapter Six

They had ridden a little way when Thea looked back.

"There are . . two soldiers behind . . us!" she said nervously to Nikōs.

"I know," he answered. "The Officer insisted that we were seen home safely, and I have also arranged for them to take our saddles to be repaired."

He spoke lightly, but Thea had the idea he was glad to see they were there.

They would be in no further danger as they made their way to the little house.

She thought, although he did not say so, that he must be elated.

The Bandits who had been a menace for so long in the mountains had at last been captured.

She knew it would delight her father.

Then she remembered that she would not be able to tell him about it.

In the fear and shock of hearing the fighting outside the cave, she had forgotten that last night she had promised to marry Nikōs.

Now it seeped through her like the sunshine streaming through the trees that she would be his wife.

Then once again she was realising the penalties of making such a decision.

It made her shiver to think of how angry her father would be.

He would undoubtedly find it difficult to explain to King Otho whad had happened.

Yet she knew that whatever people might say about 'duty' love was stronger than anything else.

She loved Nikōs, she loved him with every breath she drew, and to leave him and to be without him would be a living hell.

They rode on in silence, until ahead of them she saw the little house.

She felt that the sunshine which had turned the windows to gold had a special message for her.

She knew it was a welcome because she was coming back to stay.

They rode into the yard at the back and as Valou came running towards them, Nikōs said:

"Go into the house, my darling. I will just tell the soldiers what I want them to do about the saddles, and then I will join you."

She had the feeling that he did not wish to have to explain to Valou that they had been captured by the Bandits.

She did as Nikōs told her and ran upstairs to her bedroom.

She thought, when she saw the beauty of it and the glowing colours on her bed, how different it was from where she had slept last night.

Yet all her life she would remember the joy and security of being close to Nikōs, and the wonderful things he had said to her.

"I love him . . I love . . him!" she said over and over again.

She washed and changed her blouse for the other one she had brought with her.

Then she hurried downstairs.

As she expected, breakfast was laid ready on the balcony and Nikōs was waiting for her.

He rose as she walked towards him and she saw the love and happiness in his eyes.

Because she wanted to be sure he was there she put out her hands towards him.

He raised them one after the other to his lips.

"We are safe . . and we are . . home!" she said softly.

"We are home, my precious," he replied, "and never again will I allow anything so horrible to happen to you!"

His voice was caressing and she wanted him to kiss her.

But at that moment Géza came out with a tray on which was their breakfast, and a pot of hot coffee.

Thea sat down and looked at the exquisite view below them.

She thought it was even more beautiful than it had been yesterday and the day before, but she knew it was because her whole body was pulsating with happiness.

They ate at first in silence because they were both hungry.

Then Nikōs sat back in his chair and said:

"I have something to say to you."

Thea looked at him apprehensively.

He had spoken seriously and she was suddenly afraid that something was wrong.

"It is nothing frightening," he said reassuringly, "in fact the very opposite."

Thea drew in her breath.

"I . . I thought . . perhaps you had . . changed your mind," she said in a small voice.

"About marrying you?" Nikōs asked. "I swear to you that will never happen, not until the stars fall from the sky and the seas run dry."

She gave a little laugh of sheer joy.

"What I want to say to you concerns our marriage," he said.

Thea waited expectantly.

She thought now that perhaps she would have to confess to him who she really was.

But she was afraid that if she did so he might refuse to marry her.

He would know perhaps better than she did the penalties of renouncing her rank for being an outcast among her own people.

Frantically she began to think of some name she could give that was not her own.

She knew if she invented one it might render the marriage illegal.

Then she remembered that her father had a great number of titles.

She thought it was unlikely that Nikōs would have heard of them.

She felt sure if she chose one which her father had never used, not even when he was travelling incognito, it should be safe.

As it was all passing through her mind Nikōs said:

"I have been thinking, my darling, that when we are married, as I intend we shall be later this evening, it will be a very memorable day in our lives."

"The most . . wonderful day I . . could possibly . . imagine," Thea said.

"And for me it will be a glory out of this world!"

He reached out as he spoke and took her hand in his.

"Because it means so much to us both," he said, "I think it would perhaps spoil the wonder of it if we make tedious explanations to each other about our past."

Thea looked up at him with a puzzled expression on her face.

"The only thing that matters to us is the future," he went on, "when we will be together. I suggest therefore that we think only of our love and of nothing else."

Thea's fingers tightened on him as she said:

114

"You mean . . we do not need to . . explain exactly . . who we are . . until later?"

"Much later," Nikōs said, "when you are my wife, and I have talked to you about something much more important, which is, my lovely one, love!"

The way he spoke made Thea feel again the ecstasy she had felt yesterday when they had listened to the Voivode playing his violin.

"I think it is a . . marvellous idea," she said, "but if we are married simply as 'Nikōs' and 'Thea', will . . it be valid . . ?"

"I promise you," Nikōs replied, "that I intend to tie you to me with a legal bond as well as a spiritual one, which can never be broken!"

That was what Thea wanted to hear.

At the same time it was an immeasurable relief not to have to explain who she was and why she had run away.

She thought that once again Nikōs was reading her thoughts and without her telling him so, he knew she was worried about her past.

They had this strange perception about each other.

He was aware not only of what she felt, but also of what was in her mind.

Nothing, she told herself, could be more perfect than that she should belong to him as his wife.

It would be foolish if their happiness, if not spoilt, was disturbed by the revelation that she was neglecting her duty in giving up her rank.

Her face was radiant as she said:

"When are we . . going to . . be . . married?"

"This afternoon," he answered, "when the sun will not be as hot as it will be earlier. Until then, my precious, I want you to rest."

"I do not . . want to . . leave you."

"I have a lot of arrangements to make," he said gently

"and as last night was also for me somewhat disturbed, I too intend to rest."

He looked at her for a long moment before he added:

"I shall be thinking of you, loving you, counting the minutes until you are mine."

As he spoke she saw the fire in his eyes and the colour rose in her cheeks.

Then she looked away from him, and he said softly:

"I adore you when you blush and look shy! I do not believe any human being could be so attractive."

As she blushed again he added:

"But you are not a human being, and for that matter, neither am I! We belong to the gods, to Héja, who saved us last night and will, I know, look after us tonight."

He raised her hand as he spoke and kissed it.

Then because she knew it was what he wanted after looking at him lovingly, she went indoors.

Only as she was taking off her very creased riding-skirt did she remember she had nothing in which to be married.

She thought of all the beautiful gowns that filled her wardrobe at the Palace, and she wished that Nikōs could see her in them.

Then resolutely, because she wished to have no regrets, she told herself it did not matter.

He would love her whatever she wore, as she would love him.

She got into the comfortable bed.

As she did so she thought that the birds and the squirrels on the headboard welcomed her back.

She rested her head on the pillow and knew that she was, in fact, very tired.

So much had happened and she felt too as if she had passed through every emotion it was possible to feel.

She shut her eyes and tried to think only of the music of the Gypsies and the note in Nikōs's voice when he had asked her to marry him.

116

"Tonight," she whispered, "I shall . . be his . . wife!"

The sunshine was dancing dazzlingly in the room as she fell asleep.

Thea awoke and realised that what had disturbed her was Valou's wife preparing her bath.

She could smell the fragrance of jasmine filling the air.

She sat up and asked:

"What time is it?"

"Getting on for four o'clock, Gracious Lady," the woman answered, "and on the Master's orders, I bring you something to eat."

She brought in a tray and put it down beside the bed.

Thea saw there was a bowl of cold soup, various fruits and a sponge cake as light as thistledown.

As she was eating the woman came back into the room carrying something over her arm.

"What is that?" Thea asked.

"Master tell me," the woman replied, "that you be married, and we all very happy! Master often lonely by himself."

Thea thought that was something he would never be again, but she was looking at what she now realised was a gown.

"Master say," Valou's wife went on, "that you have nothing in which be married. This, Gracious Lady, I make for my daughter. She marry next year."

Looking at what she held up Thea saw it was a wedding-gown.

Girls started when they were very young to embroider their wedding-gowns, which were often in consequence, masterpieces.

She could see that what Valou's wife was holding was as brilliant an example of local craftsmanship as the bed in which she was lying.

117

The gown was white. It was heavily embroidered round the hem of the full skirt with flowers of every colour.

The sleeves from the shoulder to the wrist and the low neck were a riot of the flowers that bloomed in the grassland and in the woods.

It was beautiful and quite different from any gown she had ever seen.

"It is lovely!" she exclaimed. "But will your daughter mind if I wear it?"

"She very honoured, Gracious Lady."

Thea did not waste any more time.

She got up and had her bath.

When she had dried herself, Valou's wife helped her into the wedding-gown.

It had been made for a girl who was not yet sixteen, so it fitted her perfectly.

She knew as she looked at herself in the mirror that Nikōs would admire her.

It was like him, she thought, to remember that she would want to look beautiful on her wedding-day.

When she had arranged her hair, Valou's wife brought her a wreath.

It had a short tulle veil at the back and the flowers were real.

They looked very lovely against her red hair and she was sure that Nikōs had deliberately chosen them in white and blue.

When she was ready, she thanked Valou's wife and a little selfconsciously ran down the stairs.

Nikōs was waiting for her in the Sitting-Room.

When she entered it she gave a little gasp of surprise.

He looked quite different and not at all what she thought of as himself.

He was dressed in fact, in conventional clothes that she had never seen him wear before.

The cravat at his neck was exquisitely tied and the only

unconventional detail was the red sash he wore under his long-tailed coat.

It gave him a somewhat raffish appearance and Thea exclaimed:

"You look very . . smart!"

"And you look exactly as I wanted you to," he said, "a goddess from the mountains and the Queen of my heart!"

At the word "Queen" Thea stiffened.

Then she told herself that it was the title she wanted, and Nikōs was the King of her heart.

She moved towards him thinking he would kiss her.

Instead he put his hands on her shoulders and said in a serious voice:

"Are you quite certain, Heart of my Heart, that you will never regret marrying me?"

"How could I? It is what I want more than . . anything else in the . . world!"

"I am giving you a last chance to escape," he said. "At the same time, if you try to do so, I am quite certain I shall stop you. I could not let you go!"

"All I . . want is to stay . . here with you for . . ever," Thea said, "and to love you so that you never become bored with me."

"That would be impossible," he answered. "Now we must go."

He took her to the door and she thought there would be a carriage waiting outside.

To her surprise there was only Isten.

She saw he had a new saddle and his harness had been decorated with flowers.

Valou was grinning when he saw them.

Nikōs picked Thea up in his arms and sat her on the saddle. Then he mounted behind her, and picking up the reins rode into the wood.

Thea thought this was how she had wanted to ride.

With Nikōs's arms around her, close to him, her lips very near to his.

She thought that no man could look more handsome, and at the same time, so authoritative.

It was the same way he had looked when he had forced the Bandits to listen to him.

Because she was afraid that her feelings for him would overwhelm her, she managed to ask:

"Where . . are we . . going?"

"We are going to be married in a strange little Church," he said, "which I hope you will come to love as much as I do."

"Is it in the wood?" Thea asked.

"It is in the wood," Nikōs affirmed, "and the Priest is a very old man whom I have known all my life."

He paused before he went on:

"He was offered a Bishopric, but because he loves the woods and the animals that live here amongst the trees, he came here to pray for them, and for people who are too busy to pray for themselves."

As Nikōs spoke they were moving slowly along a very narrow track.

The sun shining through the fir-trees threw shadows in strange patterns on the path.

As always when she was in a wood, Thea felt as if she was aware of the spirits that lived in it.

The goblins, burrowing under the ground, and the gods above them in the mountains.

As she had found Nikōs in the wood, she thought after centuries of searching for him, it was perfect that this was where she was to be married.

"That is what I think too," Nikōs said.

Thea gave a little laugh because once again they were knowing what each other was thinking.

Then ahead of her she saw the Church and knew it was like no other Church she had ever seen.

It was made of the trunks of the trees, and there were trees all around it, so that it seemed to be a part of them.

As they drew nearer she saw that there was no glass in the windows.

Most of the Church was covered in creeper with small birds of every sort flying and and out of it.

There were also dozens of little red squirrels and running on the ground were rabbits and hares.

Nikōs brought Isten to a standstill and a small boy came from the building to hold the bridle.

Nikōs dismounted and lifting Thea down said quietly:

"Now, my darling, our new life begins!"

He gave her his arm and they walked up the wooden steps into the Church.

It was empty save for a Priest standing in front of an exquisitely carved and coloured altar.

As they moved up the aisle Thea was aware of the soft movements of birds and animals.

She felt because they were not frightened that they knew she loved them.

They were blessing her marriage in their own way.

As soon as they were in front of the Priest he began the beautiful words of the Marriage Service.

When Nikōs made his vows in his deep, serious voice, Thea knew how much it meant to him.

She knew too how much he loved her.

As he put a ring on her finger she was aware that it was not the conventional wedding-ring.

It was a signet-ring which he must have taken from his own hand.

She thought later he would give her a traditional wedding-ring.

Yet she knew that the ring which had been blessed by the Priest would always be her most treasured possession.

As they knelt for the blessing Thea felt as if the whole Church was silent.

At the same time she and Nikōs were enveloped in a light that came not from the setting sun, but from Heaven itself.

When the Service was over, Nikōs led her away and they left the old Priest kneeling in front of the altar.

Thea felt sure he was praying for their happiness and that they would never lose each other.

Isten was waiting for them outside.

Nikōs gave the boy who held him a golden coin which made his gasp with excitement.

As they rode away he shouted out after them:

"Good luck! God bless you!"

There was something very touching in his young voice.

It flashed through Thea's mind that perhaps one day it would be their son who called after them in similar words.

It made her blush to think of it.

As she turned her head so that she could rest it against his shoulder Nikōs said:

"A strange wedding, my darling, but now you are mine for eternity!"

Thea loved him so much that there were no words in which to tell him so.

As if he understood and was in a hurry to get home he urged Isten to move a little faster.

The sun was sinking low when they got home and the sky was crimson and gold.

The windows of the house reflected the sky, and it seemed to Thea as if that too was part of the beauty of the whole world.

Valou took Isten from them and they walked into the house and went into the Sitting-Room.

A log was burning in the fireplace.

Now there were great vases of flowers that had not been there before.

Nikōs shut the door, then, before Thea was expecting it, his arms were around her.

"My wife!" he said quietly.

Then his lips were on hers.

As he kissed her the rapture she had felt before seemed to seep through her.

The intensity of it made her feel as if he carried her into the sun.

She realised his kiss was passionate and demanding but at the same time there was something very spiritual about it.

She knew the beauty of the Service in the little Church in the woods still lingered in his mind.

He kissed her as if he owned her, and at the same time there was a reverence about his love and it was what she too felt for him.

She not only loved him as a man who had captured her heart.

She also admired him because he was so fine and noble, and she knew too that he was good.

She thought perhaps that was a strange word to apply to him.

Yet there was no other word which could express what she felt and was in some way linked with everything in which she believed.

Nikōs kissed her until they were both breathless.

Then as the sun that had been coming through the windows died away and it was dusk he said:

"Come and have something to eat, my beloved. It is waiting for us next door."

They went into the Dining-Room and she was not surprised to see that it too was decorated with flowers.

They were all white, the table was beautifully arranged, but there was nobody to wait on them.

As Thea looked at the sideboard she realised that Valou's wife must have been cooking all day.

"How can we eat so much?" she laughed.

"Valou and his wife will be very disappointed if we do not!" Nikōs answered.

He kissed her lightly as he spoke.

Then he chose without her telling him what she would eat and put the plate down on the table.

"I am too excited to be hungry!" Thea said.

"So am I," he answered, "but they have gone to so much trouble."

She knew he was only making it an excuse to make her eat.

She tried, but afterwards she could not remember what she had.

She was only acutely aware of Nikōs looking so handsome and so different from the way he had looked before, with his artist's bow-tie and his velvet jacket.

There was champagne to drink.

But she felt it would be impossible to feel more elated than she did at the moment.

Nikōs raised his glass.

"To the most beautiful woman I have ever seen!" he said. "Someone also so perfect in every way that I find it hard to believe that at last she belongs to me!"

"You sound as if you have been waiting a long time," Thea teased, "and I know people would be shocked if they knew the truth!"

"The truth is quite simple," Nikōs answered. "I have been searching for you in this life and, I think, in a million other lives before I found you, and now I will never let you go."

"Do you think I would want to?" Thea asked.

"I have fought a thousand battles for you, I have sailed across a hundred seas and climbed the highest mountains to find you."

"I know . . now that I have been . . looking for . . you too," Thea said. "You were in my dreams . . but when I awoke . . you were . . gone."

"Now I will always be there," Nikōs said, "and I think we both realised in the Church in the wood that love is found in strange places, and not always those that are conventional."

Thea thought of her father's plans for her, and knew that Nikōs was right.

The love they had found had nothing to do with the mundane world.

It was spiritual and belonged to the trees, the birds, the flowers, the sun and the stars.

They finished their meal.

Then when Thea thought they would return to the Sitting-Room to sit in front of the fire, Nikōs drew her upstairs.

As he did so she felt her heart begin to beat excitedly.

She could feel his need of her vibrating from him.

They reached the top of the staircase.

He turned to the room on the other side to hers, which she had never seen.

He opened the door and for a moment she felt she must be dreaming.

It was so different, so entirely different from anything she had expected, from any bedroom she had ever seen before.

As she looked round she realised the walls were all hung with material.

On it Nikōs had painted the flowers that meant so much to them both, and the birds they had just left behind in the wood.

It made the room look as if they had stepped onto the flower-filled grass on which they galloped their horses.

There were flowers of every colour flaming round them. It was so beautiful that Thea could only stare at it in bewilderment.

"I think, my precious," Nikōs said, "that when I painted this I was thinking of you."

"It is beautiful!"

"And that is why you need the right background for me to tell you how much I love you!"

Now Thea could see the bed, which was very low on the floor.

It was carved in the same way as her own.

The difference was that the headboard was decorated entirely by butterflies – large ones, small ones, they flew open-winged to blend with the flowers on the walls.

"How can you have . . thought of anything so . . wonderful?" she gasped.

"I told you – I was thinking of you!"

Nikōs put his arms around her.

She realised that while she had been looking at the room he had pulled off his coat and his cravat.

Now in his thin white shirt and the red sash above his trousers he looked, she thought, even more exciting than he had before.

Because she felt shy she said a little incoherently:

"I . . I have not yet . . thanked you for . . thinking of my . . wedding-gown!"

"You looked adorable in it!" Nikōs replied. "But now I want you closer to me, and I want to see your glorious hair over your white shoulders."

He took off her wreath as he spoke.

Then he pulled her close into his arms and kissed her.

She was trembling with the excitement that was flickering through her like little flames.

He lifted her arms.

Her gown slipped onto the floor and he carried her naked to the bed.

He put her down and as she looked up at the ceiling she saw it depicted the sky.

One half of it was blue and brilliant with sunshine.

The other half was filled with stars.

She knew, now that the sun had set, the real stars would be above them in the sky.

And yet, here in this room, Nikōs had somehow captured the world which mattered to them.

A world of beauty, music and birds.

Even as she thought of it, she heard the soft sound of the Voivode's violin.

For a moment she thought she must be dreaming.

Then she realised that he was playing the same ecstatic music which had moved her so emotionally the day before.

As the melody throbbed with a passion that aroused her Hungarian blood, Nikōs joined her.

He blew out the candles which had illuminated the room before he did so.

To her astonishment, there was a faint light behind the silken walls, and in the ceiling over head.

She did not ask him how it was done.

She only knew it was so lovely, unusual, original and so exciting that it completed the wonder of the world that contained just them alone.

No-one could encroach on them at this moment. No-one could hurt them.

She knew that what Nikōs had said was true – they were protected by the gods.

Then he was kissing her eyes, her nose, her lips and the softness of her neck.

It made her thrill.

She could feel a wild passion that was irresistibly demanding seep through her.

It was the ecstasy of Nikōs's kisses. His hands moving over the softness of her skin. His heart beating against hers.

The music swirled and rose as if the notes themselves flew up to the stars and touched the moon.

Thea knew that her heart and soul went with it.

"I worship you!" Nikōs said.

His voice was part of the music which was becoming more and more intense.

Now there was a wildness and an irresistible desire.

Thea felt a longing within herself that she could not control.

She loved Nikōs absolutely, completely. She wanted to be even closer to him than she was at this moment.

She did not understand, and yet she wanted to give him herself.

She wanted to be his and no longer have any identity of her own.

"I love you . . oh, Nikōs . . I love you!"

She was not certain whether she said the word aloud.

They came from the rapture that he was giving her.

"You are mine!" he said. "Mine, Thea, as you were meant to be since the beginning of time!"

"I am . . yours! I . . want to be yours . . and oh . . Nikōs . . I love you!"

The music rose higher and higher and was carrying them together towards the stars.

She could feel the fire on Nikōs's lips and the fire within her breast.

The world was left behind.

There was nothing except their love and they were one person.

It was a long time later, when the Voivode was no longer playing and the light behind the curtains was a soft glow, that Thea whispered:

"I . . I did not know that . . love was like this!"

"Like what?" Nikōs asked.

He drew her a little closer to him and his lips were on her hair.

"It . . it belongs to . . God," Thea said, "and it is also

. . everything that I believe in and sensed was there . . if only I could . . find it."

She was thinking as she spoke of the woods and of her dreams.

She was seeing, as if she was sitting beside it, the lake where she had found Nikōs.

"We have been very privileged," he said quietly. "The gods have blessed us and we must never cease to thank them."

"How could I do . . anything else . . now that I am your wife?" Thea asked.

She gave a deep sigh.

"I never dreamt I should find anyone so . . marvellous but . . somehow . . I knew you were there."

"And I feel the same," Nikōs said, "but I was desperately afraid that my dreams would never come true."

"And now that they . . have?" Thea asked.

"I have to make sure that I am not dreaming!"

Because he was touching her she gave a little murmur.

"How is it possible," he asked, "that you can be so lovely, so beautiful, so perfect in every way?"

"That is what I . . want you to think . . but I am a little afraid you may be . . disillusioned."

"That is something I will never be!" Nikōs said. "I know that only you, my darling, wonderful little wife, could have married me as you have without explanations, without having anyone to whom you belong at the Wedding Service."

"I . . I do not want to . . think about it," Thea said. "Tonight there is . . nobody in the whole . . world but . . you!"

"For me," Nikōs said, "you fill the sky. I know that if anybody is missing you it is the gods in the mountains above us."

"When you . . loved me," Thea said in a low voice, "I

129

felt as if we were . . one with the gods . . and no longer human."

"I thought the same," Nikōs answered. "And now that my 'Ice Maiden' has melted, I am no longer afraid she will go back to the snow."

Thea gave a little choked laugh and hid her face against his neck.

"Are you . . shocked that I was . . so excited by you?" she asked.

"How could I be shocked by my own Hungarian blood?" Nikōs replied. "And I still have a great deal to teach you about love, my precious."

"That . . is what I . . want," Thea said, "and only you could have thought of the music which makes me feel very . . Hungarian!"

"I am only afraid that I might have disappointed you."

She knew he was teasing her and she said passionately:

"You are . . everything they have ever . . said about Hungarians, and now I know what the word 'Lover' really means!"

Then Nikōs was kissing her again.

Once more her whole body seemed to be filled with fire as she responded to him.

She was not sure whether the Voivode's music was still playing outside, or whether she heard it in her heart.

But there was music rising to a thrilling crescendo.

As Nikōs made her his, they were once again touching the stars.

Chapter Seven

Nikōs got out of bed and pulled back the painted curtains so that the sunshine could seep into the room.

There were two windows when the curtains were drawn back; one looking over the woods and one over the valley.

Thea saw him silhouetted against the morning sky.

She thought that no-one could be more attractive, no man more masculine.

"Do you realise, darling," she asked in a soft voice, "that we have been married for four days?"

"I am not certain," Nikōs replied, "whether it feels like four centuries or four hours!"

He was teasing her and she laughed.

Then he came back to look at her with her red hair falling over her shoulders.

The butterflies behind her seemed part of her green eyes.

"I wonder if you realise how lovely you are?" he asked in his deep voice.

"Tell me," she pleaded.

She put out her hands to him, and he said:

"You are tempting me, but while I want to get back into bed and make love to you, I have to get up."

There was something in the way he spoke which made Thea look at him apprehensively.

"Why?" she asked after a moment.

She thought he was feeling for words before he said:

"Ever since we have been married, my precious, every-thing we have done together has been so rapturous, so unbelievably marvellous, that all I want to do is to stay here for ever, telling you how perfect you are!"

"That is . . what I want too," Thea said.

Then because her instinct told her there was something else, she asked nervously:

"What has . . happened? What is . . wrong?"

"There is nothing wrong," Nikōs said. "But I knew, my darling, we would have to face the world one day, and unfortunately it is today!"

"Today?" Thea asked. What do . . you . . mean?"

He got into bed, put his arms around her and pulled her close to him.

"I do not want you to be frightened," he said. "At the same time, I want you to do what I ask of you."

He felt a little tremor run through Thea before she replied:

"You know because I love you that I will do . . anything you ask but now . . I am frightened!"

"It may seem frightening," Nikōs said, "but I want you to trust me."

She remembered he had said the same thing when they were being taken prisoner by the Bandits.

"You know I trust you," she said passionately, "and I love and adore you. No man could be more utterly and completely wonderful!"

Nikōs's arms tightened. Then as if he forced himself to speak he said:

"I have had a message which makes it imperative for me to see my family."

Thea drew in her breath and stifled a cry of horror.

"I think therefore," Nikōs went on, "while I tell my family about you, you must tell yours about me."

"T . . tell my . . family?" Thea faltered.

Nikōs smiled.

"I suppose sooner or later we have to be frank with each other. It seems incredible that I have no idea what your name was before you became my wife!"

"Does it . . matter?" Thea asked.

"It is something we both have to do sooner or later," Nikōs replied quietly.

There was a long silence and Thea knew that he was willing her to do what he wished.

Because she could not bear to disappoint him, she said after a moment in a very small voice:

"What . . am I to do?"

"I want you to tell them," Nikōs replied, "and I think, my darling, that you came here from Gyula."

He saw Thea start and he went on:

"Tomorrow, after I have arranged everything and done what I have to do, I will come to Gyula and meet your father and mother."

Now Thea did give a little cry of protest, and Nikōs said:

"Do not be afraid. If they are angry I will placate them. Do not tell them tonight that we are married, but leave me to bear the brunt of their anger."

"They will be . . furious!" Thea murmured.

"Just make your apologies for having been away for so long," Nikōs answered, "and trust me to do what is right when I arrive."

"How . . how will you know where to . . find me?" Thea asked.

As she spoke she knew she was shrinking from telling him who she was.

If he was going away from her, perhaps when he had time to think it over, and she was not there, he would be sorry that they were married.

"Leave everything until tomorrow," Nikōs said as if he read her thoughts.

He thought for a moment, then he said:

"Meet me outside the town, then we will go together to confess what has happened and hope that your family will forgive us."

He smiled as he spoke, but Thea wanted to say that it was no laughing matter.

She could imagine the contempt with which her father would treat any commoner when she had married.

She also had a vision of them both being thrown out of the Palace and humiliated in front of the Courtiers and the servants.

Then as if everything was decided Nikōs turned her face up to his and kissed her.

For a moment, because she was perturbed, she did not respond until inevitably she felt her heart throbbing with excitement.

The flamers of sunshine ignited within her and turned into fire.

Then, as the sun came flooding in to turn Thea's hair to a shining glory, everything else was forgotten.

Nikōs was kissing her, touching her, and how was it possible to think of anything else?

Her whole body responded to his and they were in a dream-world.

There was only themselves and the beauty of the gods.

Thea rode over the grassland.

She knew that within a few minutes she would have her first sight of the City and the Palace white and majestic standing above it.

She had the terrifying feeling that she was leaving her happiness behind her.

Nikōs, before he saw her off, had held her close in his arms.

"You are not to be frightened," he ordered, "you are to think of our love, and know that because you are my wife, no one can take you from me."

134

"Y.you are . . sure of that?"

"Absolutely certain!" he said. "Once again, my perfect little wife, I ask you to trust me."

He kissed her until she knew she would have gone down into hell itself if he had asked her to do so.

When she had ridden away she did not look back, because it might be unlucky.

She was aware that Isten was waiting for Nikōs, and also he was dressed in conventional riding clothes.

Again his artist's bow had been discarded, and his white stock was neatly tied around his neck.

His polished riding-boots shone like mirrors.

She clung to him, terrified that once they were parted she would never see him again.

"You . . will be . . safe?" she asked in a trembling little voice.

"I promise you there will be no Dragons, no Bandits, nothing to harm me until I come to you tomorrow."

"At what time?"

He thought for a moment, then he said:

"At about four o'clock. Where will you meet me?"

"In the meadowland just before you reach the bridge which leads into the City," she answered.

"You promise me you will be there?"

"That is the question I was going to ask you," she replied.

He kissed her again and lifted her up onto Mercury's back and she rode away.

"I love him! I love him!" she said over and over again to herself.

She was still saying it three hours later as she crossed the bridge where she would meet him tomorrow.

She rode back to the Palace and when she entered through the main gate the sentries came to attention.

She was sure they were looking at her curiously.

She felt certain that by this time everybody in the Palace was aware that she had disappeared.

Because she was nervous, she did not go up to the front door but rode round to the stables.

The Head Groom came hurrying as soon as he saw her.

"Your Royal Highness!" he exclaimed. "You're back! Everyone's been very worried about you in case you'd had an accident!"

He looked at Mercury and Thea said:

"No, we are both quite safe."

She dismounted and walked into the Palace by a side-door.

She went upstairs to her bedroom and rang for her maid.

"Your Royal Highness!" Martha exclaimed. "How can you have given us such a fright? Where have you been?"

While she was changing her clothes Martha was reprimanding her as she had when she was a little girl, and it was all so familiar.

She still had to face her father however, and she was aware that it was going to be a difficult confrontation.

At this time of the day he would be in one of the State Rooms, dealing with the affairs of the Nation, and surrounded by his Statesmen and *Aides-de-Camp*.

She went first to see her mother.

The Queen, who was never in very good health, was resting in one of the window-seats of the Drawing-Room.

She gave an exclamation of surprise when she saw Thea, then said:

"Dearest, where have you been? We have been so worried, and your father is very angry. I became dreadfully apprehensive when we could not find you."

"I am sorry Mama, if I have upset you," Thea said, "but I think you can guess why I ran away."

The Queen sighed.

"I knew you had no wish to marry King Otho, and

when I saw him I could understand exactly what you were feeling."

Her mother was so kind that Thea felt the tears come into her eyes.

"I am sorry, Mama, but I could not marry an old man like that!"

"I know, dearest, but your father thought it was for the good of the country."

"Is he still very angry?"

"He was at first," the Queen replied, "then he thought you must have had an accident. Yesterday he sent out some officers we can trust to look for you, but they came back in the evening to say that although they had ridden a long way, they could not find you."

The Queen smiled.

"I thought you would be with one of your old Governesses but Papa did not think of that, so I did not suggest that was where they might look."

Thea laughed.

"Oh, Mama, you are so kind, and you do understand what I was feeling."

The Queen sighed.

"It is the penalty for being Royal."

"Does Papa still expect me to marry King Otho?"

The Queen looked at the door as if she did not wish to be overheard. Then she said:

"He has not said so, but I have the idea that he has now realised the impossibility of such a marriage. Try not to upset him now that you are back."

Thea kissed her mother again, then went to find her father.

Because it was now nearly luncheontime, she thought he would have moved into his Study in their part of the Palace.

She was right, and when she opened the Study door he

was standing at the window looking out onto the flower garden.

"Good morning, Papa!"

He turned sharply when she spoke, and she saw an expression not of anger, but of relief on his face.

"Thea, you are back!"

She ran towards him, put her arms around his neck and kissed his cheek.

"I am sorry, Papa, if I have upset you."

"Where have you been, you naughty girl? I thought you might have had an accident or got into danger of some sort."

Thea knew that was true, but she could not tell him about the Bandits.

"I am back now," she said, "and I am very sorry if I worried you."

"I am really very angry," the King said.

But there was a note in his voice that was more like relief.

In fact, they were all so relieved that she was home that, surprisingly, they did not question her as to where she had been.

They accepted her mother's supposition that she had been with one of her old Governesses.

Only after dinner, when they talked about everything that was happening in Kostas and read Georgi's letters did Thea relax.

It had all passed off so much better than she had dared hope.

Yet she wondered what they would feel tomorrow when she confessed that she had been married without their permission to a commoner.

'Perhaps they will forgive me,' she thought.

Then she knew that as far as her father was concerned that was unlikely.

138

Because her mother always went to bed early, Thea retired soon after dinner.

"Goodnight, Mama," Thea said, kissing her affectionately.

"Goodnight, my dearest, I am so happy to have you home again."

Her father said much the same thing, and made Thea feel even more guilty.

"I shall have a lot more to say to you tomorrow," the King added, "and no more naughtiness – do you understand?"

"Yes, Papa."

"That is a good girl! The Palace seems very empty when you are not here."

Thea drew in her breath.

As she went up to her bedroom she wondered how she could bear to hurt them.

Then she knew that nothing mattered except Nikōs.

She belonged to him. She was part of him.

Perhaps one day they would forgive her, especially if she had a baby who would be their grandchild.

It was a long time before she went to sleep, and she kept thinking that even her mother would find it hard to sympathise when she learned of the way she had behaved.

"Help me, help me," Thea found herself praying to God who had blessed their marriage.

She also prayed to Héja even though he was not worshipped by the people of Kostas.

But he was a god of the country to which Nikōs belonged and she knew that in the future He would play a very special part in her life.

Finally she fell asleep, wanting the night to pass quickly so that she could be with Nikōs again.

She had told her maid Martha not to call her very early.

She had known that the long ride home and her anxiety

as to how her father would behave had made her exhausted.

She wanted, above all else, to look beautiful for Nikōs when he arrived.

She planned which of her prettiest riding-habits she would wear.

She knew as she did so that she was really afraid that when he got home there was someone beautiful whom he had known before to greet him.

Or perhaps there was somebody whom his family wanted him to marry rather than an unknown young woman he had met in the woods.

She was still asleep and dreaming of Nikōs when she was awakened by Martha coming into the room.

She thought it was annoying she had come so early in the morning and turned over hoping she would go away.

But having drawn back the curtains, Martha came to the side of her bed to say:

"You must wake up, Your Royal Highness!"

For a moment Thea pretended not to hear, then Martha repeated:

"His Majesty says it's important that you're downstairs in three-quarters-of-an-hour."

Thea sighed and opened her eyes.

"But why? What is the time?" she enquired.

"It is nearly twelve noon, Your Royal Highness, and His Majesty says he has a special guest coming to luncheon whom you are to meet."

Thea sat up.

She wondered why her father had not told her about this special guest last night.

She hoped it would not entail one of the long-drawn-out State luncheons which would make her late for Nikōs.

She got out of bed and had her bath.

She had planned to put on her riding-habit so that she could leave without having to change again.

But as there was a special guest she allowed Martha to dress her in one of her prettiest gowns.

It was of a very pale green which made her think of the woods where she had met Nikōs.

It was made in the latest style, swept to the back with a large bustle.

It made her skin look dazzlingly white and her hair even more fiery than it was usually.

She wore a small necklace of emeralds which matched her gown.

There was a bracelet to go with it.

She did not take long in dressing and told Martha to put her riding-habit ready so that she could change quickly after luncheon.

She had chosen one of a very pale blue which was the colour of the flowers she had worn in her wreath when she was married.

She decided that this afternoon she would wear a riding-hat as Nikōs had never seen her in a hat.

Then because time was getting on and Martha was fussing she hurried from her bedroom.

She ran along the corridors to the main part of the Palace.

There seemed to be more flunkeys about than usual in the hall and also a number of the Courtiers.

She wondered who the special guest could be.

She found her father, as she expected, in the Salon which was next door to the main Dining-Room.

It was where he and her mother always received their more important guests.

It was an impressive room with a great deal of gold decoration.

Fortunately the walls were white and the carpet was blue, so that the Royal crimson did not clash with Thea's hair.

As she kissed her father and mother she saw they were specially dressed for the occasion.

"Who is this important guest, Papa?" she asked.

"It is King Árpád of Levád," her mother said before the King could speak, "and he proposed the visit himself."

"Of Levád?" Thea repeated, and wrinkled her forehead.

"He has never been to Kostas before," the King explained, "and naturally we are delighted to welcome him."

There was something in the way her father spoke and the way he looked at her which made Thea feel as if a cold hand clutched at her heart.

She remembered that King Árpád with the exception of King Otho was the only unmarried King in the Balkans.

She knew now exactly what her father was planning, and wanted to tell him immediately that such an idea was out of the question.

Then she remembered what Georgi had told her, that King Árpád was a misogynist and disliked women.

Perhaps he had changed his mind, but whether he had or not, it was too late.

She had however no wish to be alone without Nikōs when she said so.

"I must say I have never met the man," her father was saying, "although of course I knew his father. Levád is a large and important country. One of its boundaries marches with ours."

"Georgi told . . me," Thea began in a small voice, "that King Á . . . "

Before she could finish the sentence there was the sound of voices and the double doors at the end of the Salon were flung open.

The Courtiers who had been waiting in the hall now advanced towards them.

Her father and mother moved away from her, and Thea was left alone.

She knew she ought to follow them, but for a moment she contemplated leaving the Salon by another door and running away into the garden.

Then she told herself there was no need to be afraid.

She was married to Nikōs, she was his wife, and whatever schemes her father was hatching for her to marry King Árpád, they would come to nothing.

She shut her eyes for a moment, and thought she could hear Nikōs saying in his deep voice:

"Trust me!"

"He will make everything all right," she told herself.

She was sure that nothing and nobody could undo the sacredness of the vows they had made to each other in the little Church in the woods.

Her father and mother had greeted the King and were talking with him in the centre of the Salon.

It was then, slowly and reluctantly, knowing it was her duty, that Thea moved towards them.

As she did so she was saying in her heart:

"Oh, Nikōs, I love you! I love you!"

She was sending her thoughts towards him so that he would rescue her.

"And now, Your Majesty," she heard her father say, "I would like to present to you my daughter Sydel."

"I should be delighted," a deep voice replied.

Thea had already sunk down in a curtsey.

Then as the King took her hand in his she felt a strange tingling sensation.

It was so vivid that involuntarily she looked up at him.

Suddenly she was stunned into immobility.

It was Nikōs who stood there!

Nikōs wearing a uniform covered with decorations.

Nikōs looking at her with so much love that his eyes seemed to blaze with a blinding light.

For a moment neither of them could move.

Then as Thea felt she must be dreaming, King Árpád said:

"I have something important to tell Your Majesties, and perhaps it would be possible for me to do so alone."

Thea's father looked at him in surprise and asked:

"Could it not wait until after luncheon?"

"It will take only a few minutes," King Árpád replied, "and if perhaps we could go into another room with Her Majesty and your daughter I can tell you why I am here."

Thea was aware that her father thought it very strange.

There was however, nothing he could do but lead the way into an Ante-room which led off the Salon.

It was a small room which Thea had always thought was one of the prettiest in the Palace.

The door was shut behind them and King Árpád turned to Thea and held out his hand.

She moved towards him with the swiftness of a small bird seeking safety.

Her heart was beating excitedly.

At the same time she felt bewildered and could scarcely believe it was really Nikōs who stood there.

Nikōs, looking so tall and regal, so very much a King, but also the man to whom she was married.

He held Thea's hand very firmly in his, then he said in a low voice:

"I told you to trust me!"

It was impossible for her to speak, but from the way she looked up at him it was obvious that she loved him.

Then he said to her father:

"I came here today, Your Majesty, to tell you, although you may find it hard to believe, that Thea and I were married four days ago!"

The King stared at him as if he thought he could not be hearing him correctly.

Then the Queen exclaimed:

"Married? But how is it possible?"

"We met in the wood," Nikōs explained, "and we fell in love. Thea had no idea who I was, and I had no idea who she was, but we knew we were part of each other, and nothing else was of any importance."

"This is the most extraordinary thing I have ever heard!" the King declared.

Thea saw however that he did not seem to be angry.

She knew his astonishment was tempered by the knowledge that King Árpád ruled over a country that was far larger and more important than Kostas.

He could not have asked for a more prestigious son-in-law.

Nikōs was saying:

"That is the real reason, but there is another one, one which will convince the world why we were married."

Thea looked at him a little apprehensively.

He told her father and mother how, having met, they were riding in the woods when they had been captured by the Bandits.

He explained that in order to save Thea from the unwelcome attention of the younger Bandits, he had said they were married.

They had therefore left her alone.

The Queen gave an exclamation of horror, while Thea's father said:

"That was very clever of you, and I am certainly extremely grateful that you saved my daughter from those brutes!"

"Fortunately," Nikōs went on, "whenever I am living incognito at my house in the mountains which I built myself so that I could enjoy my painting undisturbed, my Prime Minister has always been insistent, although I would not be aware of it, that I am watched in case of any attack."

"So I should hope!" the King said. "You are far too important to be left unattended."

"It was something I resented, and tried to forget," Nikōs said, "but on this occasion, I was very grateful."

He looked at Thea as he went on:

"My invisible guard saw me being taken away, but he would have been powerless to tackle the Bandits by himself, even with the soldier who was with him. He therefore notified the nearest detachment of troops who came to our rescue as soon as it was dawn."

The Queen gave a little cry of horror.

"I cannot bear to think of the danger you were in!"

"Nor I," the King said. "How can Thea have been so naughty as to run away in that reckless fashion?"

Thea smiled at him.

"Are you not glad now, Papa, that I did so? If I had stayed here, I would never have found Nikōs."

"I imagine that is one of your names," the King remarked to Nikōs.

"I have five of them," Nikōs smiled.

"I have three!" Thea interposed.

"I am quite content with the one you use," he said quietly.

The two Kings then decided they would announce that Nikōs had met Thea when she had been captured by Bandits.

He had saved her and in doing so they had fallen in love.

"It is a story that our people will enjoy," the Queen said, "and I am so happy those horrible creatures are behind bars and no longer able to threaten travellers or steal our livestock."

"You may be sure of that," Nikōs said.

They then went back to the Salon and as they did so he said:

146

"I will look after Thea now, and prevent her from having such adventures in the future."

There was no chance of their being alone until late in the afternoon, when Thea asked:

"Why did you not tell me?"

"Why did you not tell me!" Nikōs riposted.

"I . . I was afraid," Thea confessed, "that you would not . . marry me . . if you knew how . . angry my father would be, and that I would be . . stripped of my rank for having married a . . commoner."

She gave a little cry aa she pressed herself against him saying:

"How could I have known . . how could I have guessed that . . you were . . so important?"

Nikōs's lips were on her forehead as he said:

"I did not tell you, my darling, because I was afraid you might be insulted at having a morganatic marriage."

Thea looked up at him in astonishment.

"Morganatic marriage?" she questioned.

"I went to my Palace yesterday to inform my Prime Minister that I was married and to ask if they would accept somebody so beautiful, so perfect as my wife and their Queen."

He gave a sigh as he said:

"I knew it would be very difficult."

"Why?" Thea asked.

"Because my Cabinet, my family and everybody from the Shoe-maker to the Blacksmith over whom I rule, have all been nagging me and begging me to marry and have an heir."

"And I thought you were an Artist!"

Nikōs laughed.

"I went off by myself to paint simply to get a little peace, and I was determined I would not have an arranged marriage to some plain, boring Princess just to please the people."

"Is that what I am?" Thea asked.

He turned her small face up to his with his finger and said:

"You know what I feel about you, and I will make it even plainer a little later."

The touch of his finger made her feel as if there was a little flame touching her skin, but she forced herself to ask:

"But you did not tell . . your Prime Minister that you were . . married. Why not?"

Nikōs smiled.

"The Bandits did me a good turn."

"The Bandits? But . . how?"

"When I got back to the Palace the officer who had taken your saddle to be mended asked to see me."

He smiled again before he said:

"He told me in a serious tone that he thought I ought to know that the saddle had been stolen from the Royal stables at Gyula!"

"But of course!" Thea exclaimed. "Papa's coat-of-arms is always marked somewhere on the saddles!"

"Exactly!" Nikōs agreed. "And that is how I found out to whom I was married."

"You were . . sure of it?"

"I had been continually told that Princess Sydel was very beautiful. My Prime Minister and most of my family had practically gone on their knees to beg me to meet you, but I had always declined."

"But . . why?"

"Because I was waiting for the right woman who belonged to me, and who was the other half of myself," Nikōs said quietly. "I felt sure that Héja would send her to me sooner or later."

"And that is what he did!"

Then she gave a little laugh.

"How could I have guessed when I fell over you and thought you were an Artist that you were also a King?"

"I thought you were a goddess or a nymph from the lake," Nikōs replied, "but all that mattered was that you were mine, and I had waited a long time for you!"

As he spoke, he kissed her.

Then as they clung together, Thea thought that all her Fairy-Stories had come true.

She had found her 'Prince Charming'. She was the other half of him as he was the other half of her.

They were together and now nothing could separate them.

Later that night when they were together in the largest and most important State Room in the Palace, Thea asked:

"How can we be so lucky . . so incredibly, marvellously lucky . . to be here . . together."

"I think the answer to that," Nikōs said seriously, "is that we have faith in our own ideals, and our belief in real love."

He pulled her a little closer before he went on:

"It was that which made you run away from the thought of being married to King Otho. It was because I knew you were somewhere in the world, if only I could find you, that I escaped from the pomp and protocol of the Palace to my little house in the woods."

He moved his lips over her skin before he said:

"I thought about you, when I painted the walls of my bedroom, and I was actually thinking of you when I was painting the lake where we met!"

"You have to finish that picture," Thea said.

"We are going there to continue our honeymoon, as soon as you have seen my Palace and met my family."

"Can we really go there and just have Valou and his wife to look after us?"

"We will be invisibly protected," Nikōs said. "I would never risk your precious life again, but to all intents and purposes we shall be alone."

"Oh, Nikōs, that is what I want," Thea said, "I want to sleep in your butterfly bed and ride with you to the little Church to thank the Priest who made me your wife."

"We will do all those things," he said, "but most of all, my beloved darling, I will make you love me more than you do already."

"That is impossible!" Thea said.

Yet as his hand touched her body she felt a wild excitement moving like fire from her breast to her lips.

She knew she was loving him more than she had done yesterday or the day before.

It was a love that would grow and intensify not only on their honeymoon, but for the rest of their lives.

It was a love which came from God; a love too which was part of the mountains, the flowers, the music of the Gypsies, the butterflies and the birds.

It was a love they would give to their children and to all those over whom they ruled.

Without love the world was empty.

With it, it was filled with sunshine and fire, and the stars which were in themselves the light of God.

OTHER BOOKS BY BARBARA CARTLAND

Romantic Novels, over 400, the most recently published being:
The Earl Escapes
Starlight Over Tunis
The Love Puzzle
Love and Kisses
Sapphires in Siam
A Caretaker of Love
Secrets of the Heart
Riding to the Sky
Lovers in Lisbon
Love is Invincible
The Goddess of Love
An Adventure of Love
A Herb for Happiness
Only a Dream
Saved by Love
Little Tongues of Fire
A Chieftain Finds Love
The Lovely Liar
The Perfume of the Gods
A Knight in Paris
Revenge is Sweet
The Dream and the Glory
(In aid of the St. John Ambulance Brigade)

Autobiographical and Biographical:
The Isthmus Years 1919–1939
The Years of Opportunity 1939–1945
I Search for Rainbows 1945–1976
We Danced All Night 1919–1929
Ronald Cartland (With a foreword by Sir Winston Churchill)
Polly – My Wonderful Mother
I Seek the Miraculous

Historical:
Bewitching Women
The Outrageous Queen
(The Story of Queen Christina of Sweden)

The Scandalous Life of King Carol
The Private Life of Charles II
The Private Life of Elizabeth, Empress of Austria
Josephine, Empress of France
Diane de Poitiers
Metternich – The Passionate Diplomat
A Year of Royal Days

Sociology:
You in the Home
The Fascinating Forties
Marriage for Moderns
Be Vivid, Be Vital
Love, Life and Sex
Vitamins for Vitality
Husbands and Wives
Men are Wonderful
Etiquette
The Many Facets of Love
Sex and the Teenager
The Book of Charm
Living Together
The Youth Secret
The Magic of Honey
The Book of Beauty and Health
Keep Young and Beautiful by Barbara Cartland and Elinor
Glyn
Etiquette for Love and Romance
Barbara Cartland's Book of Health

Cookery:
Barbara Cartland's Health Food Cookery Book
Food for Love
Magic of Honey Cookbook
Recipes for Lovers
The Romance of Food

Editor of:
The Common Problem by Ronald Cartland (with a preface by
the Rt Hon. The Earl of Selborne, P.C.)
Barbara Cartland's Library of Love

Library of Ancient Wisdom
Written with Love Passionate love letters selected by Barbara Cartland

Drama:
Blood Money
French Dressing

Philosophy:
Touch the Stars

Radio Operetta:
The Rose and the Violet (Music by Mark Lubbock). Performed in 1942.

Radio Plays:
The Caged Bird: An episode in the life of Elizabeth Empress of Austria. Performed in 1957.

General:
Barbara Cartland's Book of Useless Information with a Foreword by the Earl Mountbatten of Burma.
(In aid of the United World Colleges)
Love and Lovers (Picture Book)
The Light of Love (Prayer Book)
Barbara Cartland's Scrapbook
(In aid of the Royal Photographic Museum)
Romantic Royal Marriages
Barbara Cartland's Book of Celebrities
Getting Older, Growing Younger

Verse:
Lines on Life and Love

Music:
An Album of Love Songs sung with the Royal Philharmonic Orchestra.

Film:
The Flame is Love

Cartoons:
Barbara Cartland Romances (Book of Cartoons) has recently been published in the U.S.A., Great Britain, and other parts of the world.

Children:
A Children's Pop-Up Book: 'Princess to the Rescue.'

Barbara Cartland
A Hazard of Hearts £2.99

Serena looked at the Marquis of Vulcan in astonishment and was
suddenly aware her knees felt very weak.
'Are you afraid of love, or merely of – me?'
'Of both,' Serena replied . . .

Her freedom lost on the turn of a card, Serena is bound by a debt of
honour to marry Justin Marquis of Vulcan, a heartless cynic and the
most handsome man she had ever seen.

Accompanying Justin to Mandrake, his ancestral home, Serena enters
a house of evil ruled by his mother, the imperious Marchioness of
Vulcan, and encounters a hatred such as she had never known.

Learning by chance the dark secrets of this strange family, Serena
becomes trapped in a world of smugglers, highwaymen, gilded salons,
subterranean passages, abduction and – murder!

There was much to hate at Mandrake yet the outcome of a duel
sends Serena on a headlong gallop through the gathering darkness.
Would her ride to Justin be like her love – in vain?

Barbara Cartland
A Revolution of Love £1.99

"Help! Help me . . . please . . . help me!" Drogo looked up in astonishment and saw the figure of a woman. She was hanging from a rope down a high wall beside which he was walking . . .

Hotly pursued by Russian agents, Drogo Forde escapes from Afghanistan into neighbouring Kozan after completing a highly secret mission. Even then safety eludes him as revolutionaries storm the royal palace in an orgy of violence.

Now Drogo faces two problems. How to safeguard his vital information, and, equally important, how to protect the lovely Thekla who entered his life in such a very unconventional manner – before revealing her true identity.

An old cargo boat seemingly offers the only safety, the price a marriage of convenience that swiftly blossoms into the rapture of a shared love. The days and nights are bitter sweet for danger lurks at their journey's end, and heartbreak too, for how could a commoner be allowed to marry a Princess of Royal blood?

Barbara Cartland
The Temple of Love £1.99

When they came to the stone carving of the King, Sarida pulled back
the vines so that the Duke could see his own face . . .

To avoid an importunate mistress, the Duke of Inglebury undertakes
a special assignment for the Viceroy of India and travels incognito into
the heart of Java in search of an ancient Buddhist temple.

There he encounters its self-appointed guardian, Sarida, a lovely
English girl caring for her invalid father. She shares the Duke's
astonishment at finding he bears an uncanny resemblance to the
sculpture of a Hindu King with herself in the likeness of his Princess.

Time is precious, for the treasures of the Temple are threatened by
thieves and Sarida's virtue is under siege from the licentious Dutch
colonel of the local garrison. There are many dangers to be overcome
before Sarida and the Duke can share a love that came from eternity
and would go on to eternity.

All Pan books are available at your local bookshop or newsagent, or can be ordered direct from the publisher. Indicate the number of copies required and fill in the form below.

Send to: **CS Department, Pan Books Ltd., P.O. Box 40, Basingstoke, Hants.   RG21 2YT.**

or phone: 0256 469551 (Ansaphone), quoting title, author and Credit Card number.

Please enclose a remittance* to the value of the cover price plus: 60p for the first book plus 30p per copy for each additional book ordered to a maximum charge of £2.40 to cover postage and packing.

*Payment may be made in sterling by UK personal cheque, postal order, sterling draft or international money order, made payable to Pan Books Ltd.

Alternatively by Barclaycard/Access:

Card No.

Signature:

Applicable only in the UK and Republic of Ireland.

While every effort is made to keep prices low, it is sometimes necessary to increase prices at short notice. Pan Books reserve the right to show on covers and charge new retail prices which may differ from those advertised in the text or elsewhere.

NAME AND ADDRESS IN BLOCK LETTERS PLEASE:

....

Name ————————————————————————

Address ————————————————————————

————————————————————————————

————————————————————————————

————————————————————————————

3/87